MW01633639

EROS IN ORBIT

EROS IN ORBIT

A Collection of
All New Science Fiction
Stories About Sex

edited by
Joseph Elder

TRIDENT PRESS

NEW YORK

Published by Trident Press
A division of Simon & Schuster, Inc.
Rockefeller Center, 630 Fifth Avenue
New York, New York 10020

SBN 671-27102-4
Library of Congress Catalog Card Number: 72-96813
Designed by Jack Jaget
Manufactured in the United States of America
By The Book Press, Brattleboro, Vt.

1 2 3 4 5 6 7 8 9 10 11 12 13 14 15

Contents

Preface

"Is there sex after death?" asked the title of a recent film. An irrelevant question perhaps, but let us hope the answer is in the affirmative. In a similar vein, and in connection with the present collection, we might well ask, "Does sex have a future?"

This is a more legitimate question and not at all facetiously intended. To be sure, the pleasures of the flesh have been with us since Genesis and presumably will survive until Armageddon. Or will they? And if they do, will they assume form and content different from the familiar, the tried-and-true aspects of carnal love? Will the sex of the future be better? worse? or simply different?

No one seriously denies that we are undergoing, and have been for more than a decade, a Sexual Revolution. The Uptight Generation of the Fifties gave way to the Swinging Sixties, and the Seventies promise even greater freedom from the inhibitions of the past. We live in an age of the

Pill, of singles bars, of bra burnings, of nude legitimate theater, of topless waitresses, of Masters and Johnson, of male centerfolds in *Cosmopolitan,* of *The Sensuous Woman* (*Man, Couple, Mouth,* ad nauseam), of encounter groups, of communal marriage, of Gay Lib, of Anything Goes. Without imposing moral judgment on these various phenomena, we may well wonder, Where will it all end? Where, oh, where is this flurry of fornication, this profusion of pornography, this surfeit of sensuality taking us? To some new garden of earthly delights or to a plastic paradise of instant sensation and loveless coupling?

While the social scientist continues to ponder these questions, it seems high time that the science fiction writer had his innings. Sex, being the basic human urge it is, has always been the province of the writer, of the artist of every description, and so it is odd that the science fiction writer has remained mum on the subject. It occurred to me that he (until someone comes up with something better than the absurdly artificial pronoun *te,* I shall risk the ire of my feminine readers and cling tenaciously to the chauvinistic *he* to encompass both genders) might well have something fresh to contribute to our understanding of the age-old itch and of its potentialities. Thus are science fiction anthologies conceived.

On second thought, it is not so strange that science fiction has largely ignored sex. A very few writers in the field (Philip José Farmer and Marian Zimmer Bradley come to mind) have beaten the erotic path for their colleagues, but even fewer, until recently, have followed. Why should this be so? For one thing, the primary concern of science fiction has always been technology and its impact upon people. Throughout most of its modern history, science fiction has dealt with machines. Well, don't machines have an impact on people? Is not man (yes, that includes woman) a sexual being? Do machines, therefore, not impinge upon man's sexuality? Of course they do. Why, then, the reticence of so many writers of skill and perception (and no field of literature has produced so many in recent years as science fiction) to face head-on so fundamental and indispensable a part of all our lives?

Part of the answer lies in the puritan tradition of our society, but this, as we have noted, is a tradition subject to attack and utter breakdown on all fronts. Science fiction has simply been a little slow on the uptake to acknowledge that Something Is Happening, But You Don't Know What It Is, Do You, Mr. Jones? And this is quite understandable when we consider that science fiction as a genre has been largely confined to so-called family magazines. Yes, these magazines long ago projected an aura of titillation. Many of us of a certain age remember fondly the clandestine thrill of those *Weird Tales* covers with their Exotic Martian Lovelies in brass-bound brassieres struggling against the advances of Multi-Tentacled Horrors. What these M-THs would actually do with the EMLs was entirely a matter of conjecture. Sexual intercourse seemed a remote possibility, more likely a physiological impossibility, but the potential was there, though never realized, of course, in the pages of the pulps.

Now the pulps have long since faded, and only a handful of legitimate science fiction magazines remain, most of them in deep trouble. Like other magazines, they have suffered the inroads of television and paperback books on the attentions of the entertainment consumer. They pay their contributors scarcely more, in some cases no more, than did their pulp ancestors. And more important, they are still family magazines, subject to the strictures of the postal department, the moral code of the silent majority, the wrath of advertisers, the timidity of editors, the puritanism of publishers. It is no wonder that science fiction failed to keep pace with Changing Times.

Nor is it any wonder that writers in the field have sought new outlets. More and more we hear of writers dropping out of the short story market. Why write for two or three cents a word and then suffer the indignity of the blue pencil? Why spend hour upon hour polishing five thousand perfect words when the possibility of publication let alone adequate remuneration is so remote? Why bother, when the same time might be devoted to writing a novel?

Novels are Where It's At in science fiction, make no mistake about it. Hardcover publishers, who only a few years ago looked disdainfully down their noses at science fiction, are now clamoring to sign up the Fairhaired Boys (yes, and Girls) of the field. Happily, too, these same publishers have found gold in the short story. The original anthology (i.e., a collection of never-before-published stories) proliferates. *Eros in Orbit* is one such.

Writers who eschew the waning magazine market are eager to see their shorter fiction between hard covers. Apart from the prestige, the pay is better, the respect of editors for the written word is higher, and the range of themes available to the writer is limitless. Harlan Ellison's *Dangerous Visions* and its successors blazed the trail for the wide-open anthology. Taboos fell like tenpins. The effect on science fiction has been exhilarating. Unrestricted at last, science fiction is coming to full flower, free to probe and express the full range of human reaction to the technological revolution that has so radically affected twentieth-century man and that threatens to alienate him from his environment and from himself. Sex, finally, has become a legitimate area of concern for the science fiction writer.

And what does the science fiction writer have to say about sex? Read on. The explorations that follow are various and largely disquieting. The number of stories submitted to the editor was, in a word, overwhelming. Clearly, the science fiction writer is hungry for a forum to express himself on this once forbidden topic. What proved disquieting was the fact that the great majority of submissions envisioned no new Eden but a mating of sexuality and technology that diminishes rather than enhances the act of love. The stories included here were not specifically chosen for their expression of that theme. Contributors were invited to treat of *any* aspect of sex that could not be dealt with in mainstream fiction. That many of them found despair and lovelessness at the core of future sex is, in my opinion, highly significant. The few exceptions do not detract from the fact that these writers, who are profoundly concerned with man in his society, are telling us something about ourselves, about where we are and where we are going. We had better listen to them.

EDWARD BRYANT

2.46593 *is, according to Kinsey, the average number of times per week that the average American makes it.* (Make. *Definition 25 in* The Random House Dictionary of the English Language *is "to go or travel at a particular speed.") Some of us now, we travel faster and more. That figure was likely for 1950 or maybe 1960. Probably not 1970. Certainly not 1980.*

Would it be sophomoric to suggest that the ".46593" might refer to oral-genital contact without penetration? No doubt.

But to things poetic:

> Against the haloed lattice-panes
> The bridesmaid sunned her breast;
> Then to the glass turned tall and free,
> And braced and shifted daintily
> Her loin-belt through her cote-hardie.
>
> —D. G. Rossetti, The Bride's Prelude

Holy Christ the Redeemer, talk about soft-core!

"She's delightfully realistic and appealing. Needs no batteries. The doll that actually plays with you. She never gets tired, you can play for hours. She 'comes alive' when you blow the magic bunny-locket whistle. Put her on her bouncy bunny and blow the whistle—she sways back and forth, stops all by herself. Take her off and whistle—she waves her arms and legs, rocks from side to side like a lively tot. She has a mind of her own! Put her in her chair and show her the pictures on the magic slate. If she likes something she jumps up and down with joy—if she doesn't, she shakes her head 'no.'"

Good girl, Shirl.

If you'd lived beyond the sixth moon landing, could you have imagined anything more bizarre than what I'm about to discuss? Well, unusual. No? Confused? What the hell, it was a natural extension of the marriage manuals, an infinite variety.

No, clown, I'm not talking about the sixth moon landing. The sixth could have been the nine hundredth for all it arrested the imagination of the man on the street. Besides, a man with sickle blades welded to the hubcaps of his Volkswagen Variant had just killed eleven people in California. You had to expect popular distraction.

Now, the natural extension of the marriage manuals, etc. Imagine a couple together on the bed. Assign faces if you wish, the more familiar the better. Let's maximize identification.

Though they haven't been to church since their parents took them instead of sending them, they've assumed the missionary position. (Got the faces yet? Come on! Top or bottom—exercise your favorite fantasy.) King of the dichondra, Mr. M was—not ten minutes ago—fertilizing the tiger lilies in the back yard. Mrs. M was lightly starching Mr. M's shirts. The article said passion ought to be spontaneous.

"Oh. Ohhhh. Uh." Mrs. M feels it's expected of her to vocalize her passion. She is naked.

Mr. M wears a lightweight wireless FM headset. Adapt your eyesight to electromagnetic spectra. Trace the waves back to the transmitter plugged into the electrical socket behind the bed table. Track further to the cassette recorder humming erotically. Listen in:

"The clitoris is the homologue of the male's penis. As you feel it now, the shaft may measure something over one inch in length. Move your index finger along the inner surface of the labia minora, ending each digital stroke against the clitoris. Bear in mind that this is completely normal activity, eventually terminating in . . ."

Can you appreciate the quality of recording? Note the vibrant measured cadence, the dispassion of a newscaster announcing this week's body counts in Malaysia.

"Ohhhhh." Mrs. M screws her eyes tightly shut, except when she glances up to check her husband's depth of involvement.

Mr. M's eyes are also closed, except when he glances anxiously down to reassure himself of the height of Mrs. M's ecstasy.

Enough, enough. I hate this Dickensian feeling of drawing you ahead like the Ghost of Christmas Future.

It ain't even Christmas, Carol.

"Just imagine—this doll's so talented she can do something most people can't. Just clap your hands! Does other things too: picks up her bottle to drink, raises her arms to come to you, even plays peek-a-boo. She's sixty-two inches tall with fully jointed body, has big blue eyes, rooted hair, and lifelike vinyl body. Wears . . ."

False hair for the female pudenda. Merkins. It was a sellers' market among the Southern California survivors after the nuclear plant at San Onofre went.

On the read-out console of a third-generation IBM 6040. Where else would you seduce a cybernetic sub-systems analyst (B.S.; M.S., Michigan State University, 1977–78; Ph.D., Massachusetts Institute of Technology, 1981; and her eyes are the smoky green of Brazilian topaz)?

"I never saw you before," she murmurs. "What the hell are you?"

Gallantly I fold my jacket to slip beneath her hips. "I'm a writer," I say. Truthfully, I'm an advertising copywriter employed by the largest toy manufacturer in the Midwest. I'm on hand whenever your kid has a birthday or is anticipating a Christmas: "One of the many Leisure Toys. Have you played with all of them?"

"Toys?" She laughs. "Delightful."

"I'm sorry, I was—"

"—thinking out loud." She smiles as her fingers jig over the keyboard. "I was going to program Ravel's 'Bolero.' Instead, I think we'll hear 'March of the Wooden Soldiers.' "

Do you realize how many dead soldiers are airlifted off the battlefield with hard-ons?

"Adorable baby puts her chubby hand to her lips and throws you a big kiss, with kissing sound! Just pull the string on her back; no batteries needed. She's soft and cuddly, has foam-filled cotton body. Lifelike vinyl head and hands, rooted hair, sleeping eyes with long lashes. Eyelet-embroidered playsuit."

Alloplastic vaginas?

"I'm a modular lover," she says.

"No need to be egotistic," I reply.

"*Modular*, you ass! I believe in modular love affairs."

Christ. I don't like a lot of talk while I'm doing it.

"I plug lovers in. I take them out." She bares lovely teeth and moves faster around me.

Instant circuits overload and I— Ohhh— Holy—

Ever do it on horseback, Doris? Swinging to Banbury Cross?

"Susie with twist 'n' turn waist is an all-action fashion doll with wonderful mobility. She twists and turns from the waist

to pose in many different positions. She has eyelashes, bendable legs, rooted hair."

I watched my niece and her little friends playing on the carpet. Six G.I. Joes were gang-raping a Barbie. It was not pleasant.

Ken might have done something, but he was occupied with Stacey.

Out in the back yard my nephew was almost finished. The G.I. Joes had killed the last of the civilians. He scooped them into a mass grave beneath the rosebush with his Tonka Toy bulldozer.

It's only a toy, Joy.

Brown-haired woman with caramel nipples lies quietly for the moment, nascent liquids boiling below the skin. She unplugs me, gentle disengagement, but handles my softness with firmness. "I'll want it again soon."

And I'll want hers again soon. I grow older, a decade more. I want a woman less frequently; but when I do, the desire is no less intense than in my youth. For now, rest, and the recharge of storage cells.

"Tell me poetry." She had no time for it before.

"Which?"

She flops over on her belly, a soft brown otter stretched luxuriously. "Love poet." She contemplates the blank readout. "No Lawrence, no Levertov, no Kandel or Patchen. No McKuen."

I say, "I know. One of my favorites:

"I caught this morning morning's minion, king-
  dom of daylight's dauphin, dapple-dawn-drawn Falcon, in his riding
  Of the rolling level underneath him steady air, and striding
High there, how he rung upon the rain of a wimpling wing—"

"No."

I protest. "It's not about love but it feels like love—"

"No."

Fearful of next minute's denial, I try again:

"Yet, love and hate me too,
So, these extremes shall neither's office do;
Love me, that I may die the gentler way;
Hate me, because thy love is too great for me;
Or let these two, themselves, not me decay;
So shall I, live, thy stage, not triumph be;
Lest thou thy love and hate and me undo,
To let me live, O love and hate me too."

"That feels like love," she says. "Continue." She demands me with her thighs.

1990. 4.46593. Who says there's no such thing as progress? In the old days it was:

- *Fear*
- *Premature ejaculation*
- *Impotence*
- *Frigidity*
- *Perversion*
- *Inadequacy*

You've heard of them?
Now it's:

- *Light aluminum alloy skeletons*
- *Flexible plastic skin*
- *Stainless steel stroke-arm*
- *Ten-centimeter thrust along the plotted arc*
- *Stroke cycles per minute*
- *Depth of penetration gauge*
- *Appreciable frontal resistance shut-off switch*
- *Degree of lateral tumescence control*
- *Auto-lube-pac*
- *Lap counter*
- *Angle of thrust—*

Holy Jesus M&J (that's for Masters & Johnson, bubie) Christ, they've even got a model that ejaculates flavored yogurt.

No doubt for the .46593 trade.

Don't you wish you'd lived to see it / feel it?

Sorry, Laurie.

Sometimes I feel like a coelacanth. Got that? A crossopterygian fish—*Latimeria chalumnae.* Take the pronunciations carefully. Seal-a-canth. Very *good,* baby.

All the scientists thought the coelacanth disappeared 70 million years ago. They were wrong. A live one was caught in 1938 in the Indian Ocean off South Africa. Another one in 1952. It's a priceless link between old and new, between water-living and land-living animals.

Look at the fish, kiddies, ain't it ugly? But check it closer. Don't those fins look like legs?

Once upon a time, unhappiness was having dead batteries in your vibrator.

"Baby Tender Love makes little boys feel like they're real daddies! Vinyl-foam doll has skin so soft it feels like a baby's. Can be twisted and turned. Baby Tender Love can also be bathed and washed just like real. She drinks and wets, and has shiny blond hair made of modacrylic. Dressed in a lace-trimmed pink top and panties. Comes—"

When I was a baby, did my parents never hold me? There were no caresses, no kisses, no hugs or ever being cradled in secure arms. Is that why I now hunger for flesh? God, how I hate the rub of plastic and the taste of metal.

And how I grasp—

She shrieks, more startled than in pain. "Don't you ever trim your nails?"

"It's tactile," I say.

"Too tactile. Continue."

"I want to know your name," I say.

She raises her head, shaking it to clear taffy strands from in front of her eyes. Puzzlement: "So? I'll never see you again."

"I want to know anyway."

"A name has a string attached."

"Christ," I say, "I'm not a camera stealing your soul."

She smiles a few seconds before saying, "Karma."

"Oh?"

"It's a joke. You get out of me what you put in."

"Fair enough," I say.

"Now continue."

Plug in. Plug out.

Did you like the idea of having roots? Like a cypress; anchors into your life. Into school and church and community and state and country. Into family, friends, and lovers. And that was what I missed most. More than the flesh-touch alone, also the closeness of years.

But we moved. If we worked, we were transferred. If we had leisure, we traveled. Things and places became stale and we left and that was all right. But people were counted in our personal lives among things and places. They were as impermanent as paper dresses and rented furniture and modular buildings.

I'm lonely.

The intransigence of transience. Oh, shit how I hate it.

The computer room is silent, so quiet that our breathing is the loudest sound. During "business hours"—that is, when human beings are in the presence of the machine—the Muzak tape plays a background. White noise, they call it. Sea sounds, surf rushing in over rocks. Wind-wrapped mountains.

We are our own Muzak.

"Continue, oh, continue," she cries.

Plug out. Plug in.

"She's the flexible, lifelike teenage fashion doll who is jointed at the ankles, knees, hips, waist, shoulders, wrists, and elbows. This enables her to assume virtually every position of the human body—a doll that can mimic every action of her lover. Her hair is permanently rooted and styled fashionably to below-the-shoulder length. Perfect addition to your collection. Full selection of accessories available. Order below."

Charlotte, you wouldn't have believed it. Not after having come from a school like Baylor, where girls still wore long stiff formals and accepted scented corsages with a conditioned Southern disdain. Never, Carly.

But imagine it. We were in Illinois, north of you. Here's a board room in Champaign. Grown men—eleven of them (oh, and a woman; we'd been successfully pressured to take one on as a vice-president; fortuitously she was also black)—sitting around an ancient hardwood table.

Then I got up and showed them the storyboards for the new campaign. They dubiously examined the displays of tiny aerosol cans. Cautiously they circled the mnemonically cued copy.

"Feminine deodorant spray for dolls?" ventured Weingarten, of marketing.

"Believe it, brothers," said the woman. "It will sell."

Always trust the instincts of a survivor.

"Do you know any more poetry?"

I know no more poetry."

"I'm sorry," she says. "I rather liked it."

"Let's continue," I say.

2000. X.46593. So it's progress, yes.

"her to assume virtually every position enables"

"to assume virtually every position enables her"

"assume virtually every position enables her to"

You know what's coming? You even want *to know? Strike the transition set. Forget prosthetics, alloplastic vaginas, electronically enhanced dildoids, aids, inducements, augmentations. It's new, new this season. Total sensory experiences. Record, play back, buy off the rack. Masturbate yourself; punch a button, slot a cassette. No romance?*

Think of fine new words for the coprolalliac: sectional intercourse, homosensuality, psychelingus. You'll love it, won't you?

Orgasm's an orgasm. You feel it going in; you feel it coming out.

Can't we dally, Sally?

Plug in. Plug out.

Call me your module.

Darling . . . yes? Words that bind? Sorry.

"It has been lovely," she says.

Between spurts: "Continue?" I say. "Continue?"

"What are you?" She laughs. "A tank circuit?"

"Continue?"

And she rolls off me. "Pause. Need my breath."

I remember smoking at times like these, but now it's unhealthy. I recall talking, but that's not done. I remember wishing to wash my skin, to urinate, to find food in the refrigerator.

She hums tonelessly. She is white noise.

"Continue now?" I say.

"Yes." Skin between her eyes wrinkles thoughtfully. "New, different, though. I want to do it the old way."

Dearest . . . Old reflexes jump synapses long suspected unbridgeable. Have I pretended too long, I, the coelacanth? Do I still swim?

I want to do it the old way.

I want to do it the—

Christ, Christ, the desperate unreasoning panic of a shark lifted from the life-giving water; my internal organs, no longer supported, tear loose from inner walls.

Suddenly I wish, I wish, I wish . . .

But I can't.

GORDON EKLUND

Lovemaker

As silent and solid as a statue, Adrian stood near the center of the studio floor and watched the others. His eyes moved sporadically, whenever necessary, while the rest of his body remained motionless. The others were not aware that he was watching them. This amused him. The technicians—five harried little men dressed alike in colorful and casual fashions—were busily arranging their equipment at the central set in preparation for the focal scene. This equipment included two large bulky machines, closely resembling movie cameras in shape and appearance. They weren't movie cameras; they were recorders. At the base of each recorder a set of wires dangled loosely toward the floor. Later these wires would be attached to a headband, which in turn would be attached to Adrian's head. But that would not come until the scene was ready for recording, and that could not occur until Boone and Cynthia were done talking in their private and secluded corner.

Looking across the studio at them, Adrian sighed. He hated delays of this kind, when the difficulty was caused wholly by another person's lack of efficiency. In this case he wasn't sure whether he ought to blame Boone or Cynthia. At last he decided upon the girl, because Boone was his boss and paid his bills and deserved a measure of doubt, while the girl meant nothing to him. Adrian did not know why this delay should disturb him. Or any delay. He might have said that his time was a valuable commodity, but he knew that wasn't true. Time, as such, meant nothing to Adrian. He never thought in terms of the passing moment. He simply did not like delays.

He sat down, hooked his arms around his knees, and drew them close to his chin. Around him various twisting wires lay scattered across the floor like slumbering snakes. Adrian avoided touching any of these wires. Electricity frightened him.

In the corner Cynthia continued to cry. Talking to Boone, she raised her hands—first one, then the other—and wiped fleetingly at her eyes. In the course of the previous scene, the one recorded beside the pool at the far end of the studio, she had been required to cry. So far she had not fully recovered. Perhaps it was this which most truly irritated Adrian. The script had demanded from him a maximum of violent rage. He had supplied it, but when the scene was over and in the can, he had shut himself off with a click. If he could do it, so could she. So what was the problem?

It was her first day. Plainly she was nervous working with him, and he could forgive her for that. He was the most famous artist in the industry and she had begun performing less than a year ago—he had read her history—making recordings for a man named Buckley who operated a small studio south of the city. Buckley's recordings were technically crude and aimed at a specialized but surprisingly large clientele. Many performers began their careers with men like Buckley; few stayed with them as long as a year. Adrian never had. Adrian had begun at the top. Twelve years ago, with Boone. And he had never left the top. Nor would he.

Cynthia had stopped crying now. She and Boone came toward him, stepping casually across naked scattered wires. Adrian controlled his anger.

"All right," said Boone, "she's ready now."

"I had to calm down," Cynthia said. She stood very near him, her bare thighs level with his eyes. Past her, Adrian thought he saw a technician turn to look at her. This disturbed him more than anything. Who was this man, and what was he trying to prove? Adrian decided to report the man to Boone. Probably a new man.

"I know I'll get used to it," she was saying. "Eventually. But this is the first day and I'm a little—"

"She's trying too hard," Boone said, his hands clenched deep in the pockets of his coarse heavy overcoat. "But she is good, Adrian. You think she's good, don't you?"

"I don't know yet."

"I feel, working for you—with you—I feel I have to give my best."

"Yes, I know," Adrian said. Shifting his gaze, he looked toward Boone, but Boone had already gone away. Adrian had intended to ask a question with his eyes: *Didn't you tell her? Didn't you tell her I don't small-talk?* Either Boone had not told her or else she had chosen to ignore his advice.

Cynthia said, "I'm sorry."

"Won't you sit down?" He gestured at the floor. His mind was with Boone, watching Boone, thinking of Boone.

"Thank you." She sat at his side, one hip delicately resting against him. Cautiously, Adrian drew away from her. He was not afraid of her touch. Touching was his job, but he had seen her sit on top of a wire. He was aware that electricity passed easily through human flesh.

Boone was directing the technicians as they positioned the recorders around the large central bed. Cynthia turned to watch them, staring as though she had never seen this done before. Looking at her, Adrian almost felt like telling her the truth. But he knew this was not the right time. They needed her now. If he had dared, he would have told her that she was not suited for this work. Because of her build. She was only eighteen or nineteen and not yet fat, but her figure was large and big-boned and her hips were wide and jutting. Full frames were no longer popular. Smaller, younger girls were the current fashion. Cynthia was almost young enough and she had a pale pretty face that even Adrian found appealing, and when she smiled—or grimaced—she had a way of lifting her upper lip so that the soft pinkness of her gums lay exposed to view.

"Doesn't this sort of thing ever happen to you?"

She meant her tears. He said, "Never."

"Not even when you were first starting out?"

"No."

"Why?"

"It's always been a job to me."

"But I've been you and I know—"

Adrian turned his head sharply away from her, as though something urgent had caught his attention. But there was nothing. He was allowing her time in which to drop her thought without completing it. He knew exactly what she had intended to say: That she had been he and she knew exactly how he felt. Partly, she was right. She had been he. Every woman of every age had, at some time, been Adrian. Most men too. A billion copies of his recordings were in circulation around the world. Estimating five people for each tape, that gave one a figure slightly less than the estimated world population. And Mars. There were people living there too. Though not many. Fewer than twenty thousand. And fewer than that now. Over a thousand had died on Mars the past week.

But she did not know how he felt. None of them knew that, though all of them thought they did. Once a commentator had described Adrian as the man who bled emotions the way a hemophiliac bled blood. That was what they all thought. That was what they all knew.

"I'm getting married next week. I've known him for three years. Boone said I ought to ask you. If you think it's right."

"Sure."

"Considering the work, I mean. I know you've never gotten married."

"I've never met anyone who wanted to marry me."

"Oh, no." She giggled into her clenched fist. "That isn't true."

"Oh? Think for a minute." He turned and looked deliberately at her, almost smiling. "Would you marry me?"

"I . . ." She answered hesitantly, wondering if the truth were proper. "Well, to be honest . . . no. But I'm—"

"Don't say it." He held up a hand. "Don't say that you're different, because you're not. And don't say that you know me, because you don't. And you still won't, even after we've worked together. That will mean nothing."

"I . . ." She tried to smile at him, tenderly exposing her upper teeth, then the gum, the shining glistening teeth embraced by the folds of soft pink flesh. "You know I've never heard you say so many words at a time. Next thing you'll be smiling at me."

Boone was bawling out a technician, the same man who'd turned to stare at Cynthia. Boone's belly shook like jelly and he swung his short stumpy arms like broadswords.

"It's cold in here."

"Yes."

"I'm shivering."

"It's always cold in here. See how Boone's dressed? How fat he is? It has to be cold in here. He expects the rest of us to generate our own heat."

"You really are talking," she said.

Boone had gone to the main wall transformer, where dials flashed green and buttons beeped red, like colorful stars on an electronic Christmas tree, while the machine itself gently hummed. "All right," said Boone, his soft words echoed through the vast studio like sudden drum rolls. "Let's go."

Cynthia, standing, went immediately to the set while

Adrian followed at a more dignified pace. Like the technician, he watched her rear, seeing the way her hips waggled from side to side, wondering if the motion was habit or if she was doing it deliberately for him. Adrian smiled at her.

The bed was ready. A technician came over and fastened a headband to his temples. Two wires connected the band to one of the recorders. Then the technician did the same for Cynthia. Boone remained at the wall, checking dials. He shouted at the technicians; they shouted back. Bending down, Cynthia sat primly upon the edge of the bed. It was twenty-three feet wide and thirty-seven feet long. The mattress, thick and hard, lay flat upon the bare floor.

Adrian sat down beside her.

"Anything else?" she asked.

"Whatever I make you do, do it."

"The script?"

"Don't worry about that." He tapped his forehead above the narrow band. "I know that part."

"You make it sound so easy."

"It is. For you."

Adrian always directed his own scenes after glancing at the prepared script once each morning. Lately, conforming with audience demands, his roles had been generally aggressive, which simplifies things considerably. He rarely told the other performers what a particular scene entailed; he preferred to surprise them. It was a good technique and it nearly always worked. When a scene did fail to come off, it was never Adrian's fault. It was always the fault of one of the others, and if they failed too often—as some had—then they were not brought back. Adrian saw to that. He did not like having to repeat a scene. That was even worse than a delay.

This scene went very well. It went even better than anyone had anticipated, for the girl, Cynthia, proved to be excellent. She was wonderful. Even Adrian was amazed.

When the scene was over, Adrian quickly removed the headband and went across the room. Cynthia remained on the bed, sobbing openly. Adrian looked back at her. There wasn't quite enough blood, but he didn't care. If the proper sensations of pain had reached the recorders, then that would do as well. Let Boone worry about the necessary quantities of spilled blood. Adrian knew it was not physical proof that the audience demanded, it was the sensual experience of truly felt pain.

While he cleaned himself and prepared to dress, Boone approached. Grinning, he asked what Adrian had thought.

"You know what happened?" Adrian asked.

"You bet I know," said Boone, his grin as wide as his face. "Hell, everybody in the building knows that."

"So why ask me?"

"What about the blood? Do you think there was enough blood?"

"You know how I feel about that." Adrian sealed his trousers. He ran his fingers quickly down his shirtfront, feeling the cloth coming together.

"Yeah," said Boone.

"She's the best in a long time," Adrian said. "She could be big. You're lucky you got her."

"Gina found her. She says she wants to get married."

"That'll be all right."

"Yeah, she'll change her mind."

"That's a possibility."

"Sure." Turning his head sharply, Boone quickly scanned the room. Then, seeing nothing, the girl and the technicians still clustered about the bed, he said softly, "Are you all right, Adrian?"

"I never felt better."

"The wires. I saw you were afraid of the wires again."

Adrian controlled his anger. He was proud of the way he could handle his emotions—all of them. "I've always been leery of electricity," he said.

"I was only remembering the other time. You don't . . . you don't think that you're—"

"I don't think anything, Boone," Adrian said.

"I didn't think so, but—" Boone paused and scanned the room again. This time he was searching for help. "I wouldn't have asked, but Gina . . . she told me . . . she said you hadn't been getting on too well."

"Oh?" said Adrian. "She did?"

"She said that. But . . . well, I guess she was wrong. And I'm glad she was wrong. She'll be glad too. We worry about you, Adrian. You ought to know that."

"I know that, Boone."

"Sure." Smiling again, Boone waddled away, hurrying to his technicians. Together, the men began dismantling the equipment for the bed. It was only noon, but Adrian's day was done. He never performed more than two scenes a day. It was written into his contract. Two was the limit. When he first started, he had done as many as fifteen or twenty in a single session, the girls waiting in line for turns, but working that way, there had been too many delays. Things were better now.

Wiping darkly stained cheeks, Cynthia came over. "You're going home?"

"Yes."

She borrowed his towel, wiped her legs. "Me too." She scrubbed her thighs, making them shine as if they had been polished. "We live in the same building."

"I didn't know."

"Want to walk together? You do walk?"

"I walk."

Adrian went outside. The dome was tinted pink today, meaning it was Thursday. The sidewalk in front of the studio moved slowly beneath the heavy crush of noontime traffic. Pressing himself tightly to the gathering shadows, Adrian stood so that no one could see him. A moment later Cynthia emerged. She wore pale green knitted shorts and a pair of open-toed suede boots. Her hair fell in such a way that it covered both breasts.

"Don't they—the people—don't they ever bother you?"

"No."

He led her to the sidewalk and they got aboard. Instantly he was recognized. The air itself seemed to take notice of him, pausing momentarily before rushing ahead with the wind. It meant nothing to Adrian. Wherever he went, every day, it happened. So they recognized him; that was all that it meant. They thought they knew him. They had fucked with him or been fucked by him and they thought this meant they knew him. But they seldom molested him. He was a man they knew without really knowing. And this disturbed them. It made them stay away.

A girl riding to his left started to speak. "Adrian, I want—" and he took a long stride, sufficient to insert a fat woman between himself and the girl. The sidewalk moved downhill at an awkward angle. A thousand separate pairs of knees stood rigidly tensed.

Cynthia was disconcerted. It irritated him that she could not handle this. He was sorry he had allowed her to accompany him. It was his fault for allowing her performance to impress him. That had been an error.

"This is a big one for you too, isn't it? I'm so wrapped up in myself— This is my first— Well, I forgot about you. How important it is for you."

"Is it?" he asked evenly.

"About this being your comeback." As the sidewalk turned a corner, she leaned against him, gentle strands of artificial hair flowing close to his nostrils. "How long were you out?" Her voice stroked his ear. "A year, wasn't it? Almost?"

"About that."

"Oh, well. You probably don't care to talk about it."

He shrugged, standing upright. The corner lay behind them; their course lay straight and true ahead. Cynthia was silent for a moment, but only for a moment.

"Doesn't it ever bother you? Doesn't the way they look at you, stare at you, what they know about you. Think they know. I don't see how. Do they really mean nothing to you?"

"I'm used to it."

"I suppose so, but you—"

"You'll have to get used to it too."

"Do you think so? I don't know. This part won't be the worst for me. What's worse is when I'm inside, working. You don't have anyone—I mean, outside—I know you don't, and it can't . . . carry over. When I'm in there, I don't know who I'm with, and when I'm out with him it's even worse. I have to think, ask myself, Am I acting or am I feeling? You cannot imagine. It's all one thing, same motion, so confusing. You can understand, but he—"

"Lower your voice."

"Oh, I'm sorry. I didn't—"

A man was following them very closely. Adrian could feel him back there, hovering just beyond his shoulder. Listening.

Raising his eyes, he watched the hourly headlines streaming across the roof of the dome.

WAR EXPECTED IN AFRICAN CRISIS.

DOME BURSTS IN MANILA.

MARTIAN DEATH TOLL STANDS 2,045.

BROWNS 46 SOLONS 18 FINAL.

ELIMINATE ANDROIDS SAYS SPECIAL COMMIS.

"That's horrible." Cynthia had also been reading the headlines.

"The androids?"

"Yes. Eliminating them. That's only a clean way of saying killing them. Androids are people too. It's no wonder they did what they did. I would have too."

"But you're not an android."

"Have you ever seen one?"

"No."

"I have. My uncle lived on Mars and when he visited us he brought one with him. He was important, so they had to let him do it. He was very sick and the android was the only one who knew how to take good care of him. My uncle is dead now. I talked to the android. His name was Karl. He told me—"

"*It* told you. They're not people, they're only machines."

"You don't know. They are people. I said I talked to him."

"You heard what it wanted you to hear. That's all. On the outside they can be sleek and slick and human. They can fool anyone. But on the inside, down deep, it's all electricity. Gadgets and wires and flashing lights. Empty space. Heat—but cold heat. There's no humanity there."

The news had gone, replaced by a towering full-length portrait of Adrian. Abruptly the head of the portrait turned and peered down at the city. The lips parted in a smile of delight. Sudden red lights exploded across the pale chest.

A PRIVATE DESIRE

And then:

ADRIAN

"I never thought," said Cynthia.

"Just don't look. Keep your eyes on the sidewalk. Don't give them the pleasure."

"All right," she said.

They arrived. Adrian occupied an apartment on the uppermost story of the building, a stiff straight tower, ultimately contemporary in function and design, sheer tinted glass walls and a glistening doorman, who properly bowed.

"Good afternoon, sir."

Together they entered the lobby. A dozen elevators lay open and waiting. Cynthia started for one, but Adrian turned and hurried away from her at a rapid click.

"Adrian, wait," she said. She shouted after him, "I live in 1602."

"Tomorrow," Adrian murmured.

He dashed inside the private elevator which serviced only the top floor. The doors immediately contracted behind him. He thought he heard an excited voice saying, "But, oh, wait," but he was alone; the elevator scampered up the shaft. What had she expected from him? Why hadn't someone told her? They all knew, from Boone on down. He guessed that she must know. She was toying with him, knowing far more than she chose to reveal.

There wasn't a stick of furniture in his apartment. A pale blue carpet played clashing games with the colorful inner walls and ceiling. The outer walls were tinted green glass, but Adrian always kept the curtains tightly drawn. He had thirteen rooms, but he was careful never to enter more than three. The kitchen, where he now went to dial a cup of rainwater; the living room; the bathroom. In the bathroom a full-length mirror lurked behind the door, and Adrian often went there to see himself. This mirror was the only form of entertainment he allowed himself. Once there had been his wall paintings and moving sculptures and flowered music and the tridee. But the mirror was all he truly needed. The rest was for the others.

Now he did not even want the mirror. He merely sat in the center of the living-room floor, the pale carpet flowing gently around him like a calm slumbering lake. Closing his eyes, he shut himself off. *Click.* It had taken him considerable time to develop this talent, but now it was as simple as coughing. *Click.*

When he awoke, the room was dark. He slapped his hands against the carpet, beating alternate time—four, five, six—and the ceiling ignited with rosy light. Beside the kitchen panel the visaphone buzzed darkly. Standing, stretching, Adrian went to answer.

Gina Watson, who worked for Boone and occupied Apartment 4215, peered at him with her cold, chiseled, ageless face. Narrow lips folded back to expose freshly cleaned teeth. Her gray hair, sparse as a balding man's, lay like a wreath above slender eyes.

"Where have you been?" she demanded.

"Here."

"Just checking."

"What do you want, Gina?"

"The new girl. I want to know how she's working out. I'm afraid the name slips me."

"Cynthia."

"Well?"

"Very well."

"Do you want Wanda tonight?" asked Gina.

"No."

"I thought not. Another?"

"No."

She sighed; the sound carried easily across the intervening yards of open space. "At least you don't try to hide anything from me. You've stopped that. But so soon. What has it been? Three days. Damn it. I warned him. I said it wouldn't work. It would backfire in his face. I assume you spotted her easily enough."

"Spotted who?"

"And then she had to tell you about the revolt. What a story! Her uncle! But, you understand, there was nothing I could do. To get an efficient working model you must allow them a bit of their own mind, and always they end up turning on you. I suppose you're back to thinking you're one too. The things you don't know. If we lose another year on account of this, I swear I'll have his head on a platter. Don't let her in. She's loose somewhere in the building."

"What are you talking about?"

"And try to think, Adrian. Until we can get around to you. It's my fault for waiting. I bet you've been sulking since you got home."

"No."

"Boone warned me. I should have thought. If a thickheaded fool like him can see that something's wrong—ah, well. But try to remember your birth certificate. And your mother's pictures. The record of the operation. What the doctor said. It took us a full year the last time. Shouldn't this time. You are a human being, Adrian dear. The same as me."

"You'll be coming for me?"

"Eventually," she said, sighing powerfully. She seemed more irritated than angry, more perturbed than frightened. "Later, later, later. All in good time. Go look at yourself in the mirror, Adrian. Keep yourself occupied. I've got to find her first."

The screen turned dark. A single white dot struggled briefly for survival in the center of the screen, but swiftly spreading waves of blackness flowed quickly to consume it. Before the end Adrian turned away.

Cynthia stood near the door.

"I heard," she said.

"Heard what?" Concealing his shock, he marched hurriedly away from her, turning his back. The inner hallway stretched suddenly in front of him. For a moment his feet continued to move. Then he stopped, shivering.

"I almost went in there," he whispered, pointing ahead.

"Oh, let's," she said.

He turned to face her and shook his head. "Get out of here."

"You won't help me—hide me?"

"No, I won't."

"I didn't think you would but . . . did you really think you were one too? Is that what happened to you for a year?"

"That's what happened." He stated the truth proudly. "I thought I was one. Isn't that incredible? And you almost got me started again. Are you pleased with yourself?"

"No," she said.

He stepped forward, grasped her shoulders, shook her. Like a little girl, her bright adolescent eyes peered at him from beneath dead mechanical lashes. He let her go. "When I found out last year what they were doing in the industry—introducing things like you—I naturally thought I must be one too. You see, I never could remember my past. My life begins the day I went to work for Boone, before that it's a blank. But they showed me. A doctor did. When I was twenty, I had an operation. My life was saved, but my memory was gone. They showed me pictures of myself with my mother. All sorts of things. Now I know that I'm not one of you."

"The doctor could have lied. The pictures—fakes."

"Don't," he said softly, chuckling. "I could kill you."

"Go right ahead. Please do. What difference would it make to me? Don't you realize they'll disconnect me anyway, when they catch me? All the others have gone, because of the revolt. I've stayed awake this long because of you. But now, you see, that part is over."

He looked down. The carpet moved strangely at his feet, as though each strand were an individual worm seeking the warmth of the earth.

"Shut up," he said.

"So you won't help me."

"I won't."

"They'll get you too."

"No," he said, willing to look at her now. "You nearly ruined me again, but I should have guessed. Besides, you're too fat. Nobody is going to want you. Let them put you back in the vat. You almost had me believing."

From where he stood the outer door was visible, and now he saw it dilate. A foot passed through the opening. Gina Watson entered, followed by Boone. Two massive men, dressed only in leather shoulder holsters, came last.

"All right." Gina Watson hurried to Cynthia. "What's her name?"

"Cynthia," said Adrian.

"Well, Cynthia. You're going to have to come away with me. No trouble now or we'll have to disconnect you on the spot."

"You'll do it anyway," Cynthia said. "But all right." Her face was quite impassive. She avoided Adrian's eyes. "I'm going."

She went away with the guards.

"I expected more trouble from her," Boone said. "Don't these things care if they die?"

"They don't die," Gina corrected. "Does an electric light die when you switch it off?"

"That's true," Adrian said.

Gina looked at him. "Well, now," she said. "Is everything clear to you?"

"I'm human and she's not. I guess that's all there is to it. But—why?"

"I thought it would be better," Boone said, "easier for you. But I was wrong. She was the best available. But she nearly caused you a relapse."

"The recording will have to be done over," Adrian said.

"No." Boone shook his head and put his hands in his overcoat to emphasize the point. "I don't think so. We'll edit what we have into a whole. The plot will be a bit bare, but nobody cares about the plot. You know, actually she was good—like you said, the best in years."

"There's no way—"

"An edict is expected any minute," Gina said. "They've killed at least three thousand on Mars. We're going to have to disconnect the lot of them."

"Maybe they can fix what's wrong," Boone said.

"Maybe," said Gina. "Look, Adrian, how about Wanda?"

"Yes, I think that would be fine," said Adrian.

After they left and he was alone, Adrian sat down on the carpet and hooked his arms around his knees, locking his fingers together; but a moment later, remembering how he had used Wanda to get rid of them, he got back up and removed his clothes. When he was naked, he sat down again and he remained sitting until the door opened.

Then he crouched, watching.

Wanda had her own key. She came cautiously down the hallway, using her fingers as if she were blind, almost walking on the tips of her toes. She was a young girl, fifteen or sixteen, and wore a bright loose-fitting dress that barely covered her knees. Her dark hair was drawn tightly behind her head in twin pigtails. Seeing Adrian, she smiled at him and nodded. He had never heard her utter a word. She turned to remove her dress.

"Wait," he said. "Not yet. Here." He gestured at her to sit at his side.

She did, peering straight ahead, staring ahead.

Wanda had been his girl ever since his last recovery—a month ago, two months, something like that. In fact, it had been his renewed interest in girls which had first convinced Gina and Boone that he had finally recovered. Before, there had been other girls. Gina supplied them with ease. All were quite young and always silent. He had never asked for either quality. They had simply come to him that way. When he grew bored with one, she would disappear. One day he would call Gina and ask for Gloria but it would be another girl who came through the door. Later, after he had sent the girl away, done with her for the present, Gina would call and say that the new girl's name was Nancy. So far Wanda had not begun to bore him excessively. He found her company largely congenial.

Now they sat silently together. Adrian did not bother to turn and look at her. He was waiting for something to happen. Closing his eyes, he discovered that it was much easier to wait in the dark.

He felt it now. A tiny dot of pain blossomed somewhere in his mind. Slowly, cautiously, uncertainly, it began to expand. As it grew, he tightened his fists. His brow abruptly tingled with perspiration. His fingernails cut deep into his palms. The pain was bad. It grew worse. The pain was unbearable. He bit his lip so as not to scream. He opened his eyes but could see nothing.

The pain was gone. Like a great wave, it had risen to engulf him, but now, having passed, nothing remained but the cool slumbering waters of a calm sea.

So Cynthia now was gone. Disconnected. Dead. So now he was the very last. He would never have to suffer this pain again. Not until the day came, as surely it would, when they decided to disconnect him.

Now he directed Wanda to undress. And she did.

Now, reaching over, he took her head in his hands. Now his touch was tender and caressing, gentle and compassionate. Now he could think of nothing else. Drawing her forward, he placed her head in his lap. Bending down, way down, far down, he kissed her lips. Only once.

She raised her head. He watched as her lips approached his chest. At first it tickled and he almost laughed because his senses had been made so strong, but he ignored this, lifting the girl steadily so that she soon lay cradled in his arms. Her lips and teeth continued to nibble at his chest, suckling, her tongue gliding smoothly across the hairless flesh.

His eyes were closed now. Gently his arms moved, rocking. He hummed rhythmically a snatch of song, softly so that only he could hear, an old but wordless song, for words were not important now. His lips dry, mouth cold, throat light.

He sighed .

Her face lay warmly against his chest and he centered his feelings there, then briefly allowed them to move lower, and he felt her hair fluttering tenderly against the skin of his groin.

Now up again. Now to the center—the middle—the core.

Adrian felt his own humanity, loving its sudden taste. He knew it now—saw it, heard it, sensed it truly. He was pervaded by it.

He could not doubt, for there was no reason.

His voice cracked. It shattered easily and he was forced to cry. Tasting his own tears, he found that they were no different from Cynthia's. Or Wanda's. Should they have been?

"My baby," he told the girl who suckled at his breast. "Child. Baby."

Gently rocking now.

"Wanda," she corrected.

"Oh, yes. Wanda." Eyes closed, rocking. "Adrian," he said passionately.

PAMELA SARGENT

Clone Sister

After they made love, Jim Swenson leaned back on his elbows and looked at Moira Buono. She was a slender dark-haired girl with olive skin and large black eyes. Her nose was a bit too large for her delicate face; as she lay at his side, her small breasts seemed flattened almost to nonexistence, her abdomen was a concavity between two sharp hipbones. Her legs were a contrast to the slenderness of her torso; they were short and utilitarian, well-muscled appendages that carried her around efficiently and without much strain. Jim thought that she was beautiful, in spite of her body's idiosyncrasies. Certainly she was more beautiful than the stereotyped perfection that many mistook for beauty.

She watched him with her dark eyes. Her black hair lay carelessly around her head in the green grass, her face bore a calm and peaceful smile. She reached out for his hand, drew it to her belly. In the distance he could hear the high-pitched laugh of Ilyasah Ahmal and the deeper rumblings of Walt Merton. He traced the outline of the shadows on her body, shadows created by interception of the summer sun's rays by the leafy branches of the trees overhead. The summer breeze stirred the branches, the shadows drifted and changed shape on Moira's body.

Jim removed his hand from her and got up. His penis felt cold and sticky. He pulled on his shorts and began to walk toward the clearing ahead. He knew Moira was watching him, probably puzzled, perhaps a little angry. He came to the clearing and moved toward the stone wall at its edge. The grass brushed against his feet, tickling his soles. Two grackles perched on the wall, cawing loudly at some sparrows circling overhead. As he approached, the two black birds flew off, cawed at him from above, and were gone.

Jim leaned against the wall and looked down at the automated highway two hundred feet below him. The cars sped along the road in orderly rows, punched into the automatic highway control. He watched them and thought of Moira. She had retreated from him again, hiding from him even at the moment he had entered her body. She had been an observer, looking on as he held her, sweating and moving to a lonely, sharp spurt of pleasure. She was an onlooker, smiling at him from a distance as he withdrew, her black eyes a shield between their minds.

They stood in a gray formlessness. "Moira," he said, and she looked at him, seemed to be perplexed, seemed to be impatient. She withdrew, and clouds of grayness began to cover her, hiding her legs, then her face and shoulders.

His view of the highway was suddenly obstructed. "Are you trying to ruin today too?" Moira's voice said. He pulled the shirt she had draped over his head off his face and put it on. She was sitting on the wall to his right. Her skin looked sallow next to her yellow shorts and shirt. She stared past him at the trees.

"I'm sorry," he said, "it's just a mood." He wanted to take

her hand, touch her hair. Instead, he went back to leaning against the wall. He looked up at her face. Her eyes were pieces of onyx, sharp and cold. Her skin was drawn tightly across her cheekbones.

"I'm sorry, it's just a mood," she said. "How many moods do you have? Must be half a million by now. And they're always ones you have to apologize for." Her mouth clamped shut.

Jim turned and saw Ilyasah coming toward them, black hair a cloud around her dark face. Jim forced himself to smile at the black girl.

"You were right about this place," Ilyasah said. "Nice and quiet. Ever since they reclaimed that area up north, you can't go there without falling over bodies. Something wrong, Moira?"

"No," Moira muttered.

"Give us half an hour," Ilyasah went on, "and we'll get the food out."

Jim took the hint. "Sure," he said. Ilyasah left and disappeared among the trees. The black girl had still not shaken off the remnants of her rigid Muslim upbringing and wanted to be sure no one observed her with Walt. Moira had returned to her dormitory room with Jim one evening a little too soon. They had calmly excused themselves and gone to one of the lounges instead, but Ilyasah had been embarrassed for days afterward.

"I guess we'd better watch the path," he said to Moira. "I wouldn't want anyone else to embarrass your roommate." Moira shrugged and continued to sit on the wall. She had retreated again.

He tried to fight the tightness in his stomach, the feeling of isolation that was once again wrapping itself around him. Talk to me, Moira, he thought, don't make me stand here guessing and worrying.

The dark eyes looked at him. "I'm leaving next week," she said quickly. "I'll probably come back in August, but my mother's fixing up her new studio and she needs some help." She was silent again. Her eyes challenged him to respond.

"Why?" he cried, suddenly realizing that he had shouted the word. "Why," he said more quietly, "didn't you tell me this before?"

"I didn't know before."

"Oh, you knew it before. She's been after you for a month about it, and you said she had enough help. Now all of a sudden you have to go home."

Moira hopped off the wall and began to pace in front of him. "I suppose," she said, "I have to go through a whole explanation."

"No," he said. Of course you do, he thought.

"All right," she went on. "I decided to go home a while ago. I would have told you before, but—"

"Why not? Why didn't you tell me before?"

Moira suddenly smiled. "You really don't understand, do you? If I had told you before, you would have gotten upset and tried to talk me out of it, or acted as though I did something terribly wrong. So I tell you now, so you don't have time to talk me out of it. I thought I was doing you a favor. But of course you're going to act the same way anyway."

"I want to be with you, is that so wrong?" Jim swallowed, worried that he had whined the words. "I don't like to be separated from you, that's all," he said in a lower tone.

"No, you'd rather be underfoot all the time," she said. "I can't even meet your brothers and sister. Every time I mention that I might like to talk to them, you evade the whole thing. Why?"

He was silent. He could feel sweat forming on his face and under his beard.

"I guess," she said, "you're jealous of your own family too."

He shrugged and tried to smile. "It isn't so bad," he said. "You'll be back in August, and we can—"

"No." She stopped pacing and stood in front of him, arms folded across her chest. "No, Jim. I don't know yet. I want to think about things. I don't want to make any promises now. I'll just have to see. Maybe that's hard on you, but . . ."

She sighed, then walked over to the trees. She stood there leaning against a trunk, her back facing him.

"Moira."

No answer.

"Moira." She was gone again, had said what she had to say. He could stride over to her, grab her by the shoulders, shake the slender body while shouting at her, and she would simply look at him with empty eyes.

Do I love you, Moira? Do I even know you? He stared at the girl's back, stiff and unyielding under the soft yellow shirt. Am I too possessive, too demanding? he asked himself. Or is that just an excuse, a way to avoid telling me that you can't love a freak, that it would be as easy for you to love one of my cloned brothers if you knew them, that we're all interchangeable?

Moira, look at me, try to understand me, he wanted to shout. He walked over to her, afraid to touch her, afraid to reach out and hold her. She was lost in her own world, and seemed unaware of his presence.

It was over. He was sure of that, in spite of Moira's comments about waiting until August.

She turned around and looked at him, black eyes expressionless. "Surely you realize," she said, "that I'm getting a bit sick of the newsfax guys always asking for exclusive interviews on what it's like to be with a clone, that's one thing. The fact is, you're trying to use me to prove something to yourself, to show everyone that you are an individual, that I only love you, that I'm completely yours. Well, I've got better things to do than build up your ego."

She still refused to speak. You could at least say what you mean, Jim thought as he looked at the back of the silent girl.

"Hey!" Jim turned and saw Walt Merton on the path leading into the woods. "Come on," Walt said, "we're getting the food out."

"Yeah," said Jim. "We'll be along in a minute."

Walt looked from Jim to Moira. "Sure," he said. His dark face revealed concern. He looked doubtfully at Jim, then turned and went back down the path.

"Let's go," Moira said suddenly. "I'm starving." She smiled and took him by the hand. She was hiding behind a shield of cheerfulness now: *Nothing's wrong, Jim; everything's settled.* "Damn it, Moira," he said harshly, "can't you at least talk it over, or let me try to get through to you?"

She ignored his question. "Let's go," she said, still smiling, still holding his hand.

The rain had started as a summer shower, but was now coming down steadily, forming puddles on the lawn. Jim sat on the front porch of the large house he shared with his brothers and sister. The evening air was cooler and fresher than it had been for several days.

The large house stood at the end of a narrow road amid a grove of trees. Farther down the road, near one of the other houses, Jim could see a group of naked children dancing in the rain. On the lawn in front of him his brothers Al and Mike were throwing a football around. Mike was always ready to use any excuse for fooling around and had dragged Al outside almost as soon as the rain began to fall.

Al's thick brown hair was plastered against the back of his neck and shoulders, Mike's mustache drooped on both sides of his mouth. "Whup," yelled Mike as he drew his arm back and made a forward pass to Al. As the ball left Mike's arm, he slipped on the grass and landed on his buttocks, bare muddy feet poked high in the air. Al hooted as he caught the ball. He began to run toward Mike with it, laughing as Mike got up. There was mud on the back of Mike's shorts.

Jim watched his brothers. They had not insisted that he join them, understanding almost instinctively that he needed some solitude. He had gone to the university early that morning to drive Moira to the monorail that would take her home.

He had tried once again the night before to talk her out of leaving. "I can't believe your mother needs your help with all those others around," he said. Moira's mother lived with five other women and Moira herself had been raised communally with three other children by the group. She saw her father only rarely. He had retreated to Nepal years before, emerging only occasionally to face a world that frightened him.

Moira shrugged. "She can still use some extra help," she said.

"Come *on,* Moira," he shouted. "Stop being so evasive and at least be honest about why you're really going."

She was silent, continued to pack her things. He had finally left her dormitory room, angrily telling her she could take the train from the university to the monorail.

He had relented, of course, and driven her to the monorail after all. He drove onto the automated highway, punched a button, leaned back in his seat as the highway took control of his car. He reached for Moira, pulled her to him. She watched him; her black eyes did not show him what she thought. She unfastened her blue sari, draped it on the back of the seat. Then she unzipped his shorts, crawled onto him, holding his penis firmly with one hand. He was suddenly inside her, clutching her, gazing up at her face. Her eyes were closed.

"Moira," he whispered to her. "Moira." He came quickly, and she withdrew from him and moved back to her side of the seat.

Jim shivered in the air-conditioned coldness of the car. He zipped up his shorts and looked over at the dark-haired girl. She was fastening her sari while staring out her window at the blurred scenery. What was it, Moira, he thought, a formality because you're leaving? a way of saying you still care? a way of saying *Goodbye, Jim, it's the last time?* She gave him no answer, not even a clue. Once again she had remained unresponsive, giving him no sign that she had taken pleasure in the act herself.

He grabbed her, pulling her sari from her and pushed her down against the seat. Her face was against the back of the seat, hidden from him. Her buttocks pointed up at his face. He crawled on top of her, pushing inside roughly. He pounded against her, waiting to hear her moans, waiting to see her abandon herself to him at last.

He continued to sit behind the wheel, still watching her. She had finished fastening her sari. She turned toward him, a tentative smile formed on her face. I've never reached you, Moira, he thought. At last he pulled her to him, and she lay there, head on his shoulder, her body stiff, her muscles tight. He was alone once again.

Al stumbled onto the porch, picked up his towel from the chair next to him, and began to massage his head and shoulders vigorously. "Am I out of shape," said Al. "I'm going over to the gym tomorrow. I have to go to the library anyway, so I might as well work out."

"Yeah," Jim said absently.

"Want to come along? We can play some handball."

"No." Jim looked up at his brother. "I don't think so." He looked away, sensing what Al was probably thinking: *Is it that girl, Jim? You've been sitting around for months, no interest in much else. You haven't even written any poetry for a while.*

"Well, if you change your mind," Al said. He turned and went inside the house, towel draped over his shoulders.

"Catch," shouted Mike. He threw the football to Jim as he followed Al through the front door.

Jim tucked the football under his chair and continued to watch the rain. Again he felt separated from his brothers, seeing them as others might: identical people, clones of the same man, undifferentiated and interchangeable. Some had thought that they and their sister Kira would be identical in interests and achievements, as well as exactly like their father, Paul Swenson. But Paul, who had raised them and lived with them until his death in a monorail accident two years before, had different ideas. He had encouraged the five clones to develop individual interests. Al had become a student of astrophysics, Mike was studying physics, Ed was interested in both mathematics and music, and Kira, the only female clone, was a student of the biological sciences that had brought them into existence. Jim, however, had decided to study literature. Although he had been interested in the sciences and had studied them to some extent, it was to literature that he responded most deeply. He had often thought that he was the most emotional of the clones, that he had inherited somehow, or at least empathized, a part of Paul's personality that had not been apparent to most of those who had known his father.

No, they had not been exactly like Paul. Instead, they were fragments of him. Paul Swenson had made his mark in astrophysics, culminating his achievements by laying the theoretical groundwork for a star drive that would take humanity beyond the solar system. But he had also studied other sciences, and was an accomplished violinist. In his later life Paul had written several books on the sciences, hoping to communicate what he had learned to others, and had even tried his hand at poetry. He had been honored and respected by the world until, at the very beginning of the century, he had allowed his friend Hidehiko Takamura to make an attempt to produce clones using Paul's genetic material. The scientific community throughout the world had placed a moratorium on cloning during the early 1980s, delaying any application of the procedure to human beings. The moratorium had been part of an automatic twenty-year delay period placed on the application of new scientific innovations. When that time had run out, Takamura had urged Paul Swenson to donate himself for duplication. Then Takamura and other biologists had taken nucleus materials from Paul and introduced them into eggs from which they had removed the nucleus, in order to insure that each potential child should inherit all of its genes from Paul Swenson.

The attempt had succeeded, and the world had been horrified. Legislation had been passed in the United States and Europe outlawing the application of cloning to human beings, and the artificial wombs used to nurture the clones before birth could no longer be used except to aid prematurely born infants. Newsfax sheets had made Paul Swenson out to be an egotist and megalomaniac, although in fact he had been gentle and self-effacing. The clones themselves were the subjects of stories claiming that they had telepathic powers or a communal mind. The stories had been discredited, but some people still believed them.

Jim sighed. His sister Kira, echoing Paul, often said that they all had a responsibility to use their talents as constructively as possible, to show the world that they were, after all, fellow human beings. Al, feeling the pressure of his father's reputation, did little but study. Ed had become shy, retreating from social contact. And I, Jim thought, have done almost nothing except sit around feeling sorry for myself. But don't I have the right to, if I'm like everyone else? Why do I have to do anything noteworthy? Is it up to me to prove something about clones to everyone?

He had, after all, tried to make Moira understand, and he had failed completely at that. The thought of Moira suddenly saddened him. He had been numb for most of the day and now her absence hit him at last. I would have been with her now, he thought, we would have been running through the rain together. He felt purposeless, empty, and alone.

A car was coming along the narrow road, a light green Lear model. It stopped in front of the Swenson house, and he saw his sister and a short stocky figure get out. The two raced through the downpour to the porch. Kira was laughing as she shook the water from her hair. The short stocky person turned out to be Hidehiko Takamura.

Jim wanted to get up and disappear into his room. Instead he sat in his chair and nodded to Dr. Takamura.

"What a downpour!" said Kira. "Can I get you something—a beer maybe?"

"Better make it tea," Dr. Takamura replied. "And I think I'll sit out here. I've been inside all day."

Kira looked at Jim. "I'll have some too," he said. She hurried into the house.

Jim looked over at Dr. Takamura as the older man seated himself. The man was still here at the university, still working at the same research center that had produced the clones, and now Kira was studying with him. Jim shuddered. He usually felt uneasy around the original participants in the experiment. He could never be sure whether they regarded him as a subject or were trying to recapture their friendship with Paul.

"How's everything, Jim?" said Dr. Takamura. The older man still retained a youthful appearance and was active, in spite of being in his seventies. "I haven't seen you for a while."

"I haven't been around the house much," said Jim.

"I have seen you from a distance, wandering around the university with a very attractive young woman."

"Oh. Moira," Jim said. He paused, thinking he should say more. "I met her last winter. I was at home here, tuned in to a lit discussion, and we got into a debate. Then after the discussion was over, we stayed on the screen, just talking, so finally I asked her where she lived, and I went over to her dormitory. She's gone home until August," he finished lamely.

Kira returned and sat down next to Dr. Takamura. "Ed'll bring the tea out," she said. Jim looked at her face—his face, only more feminine—high cheekbones, large green eyes. She looked back, eyes questioning him: *Everything all right, Jim?* He tried to smile back at her.

"We were just discussing the young woman I've seen Jim with," said Dr. Takamura. Kira appeared startled. She brushed some of her thick brown hair off her face and leaned forward. "You know,"' Dr. Takamura went on, "she resembles a girl Paul was seeing when he was about your age, when we were both at Chicago. Rhoda something, her name was. She left for Israel a couple of years later. He was very serious about her for a while."

Jim began to feel uneasy. Kira seemed to sense his mood.

"It sure is raining," she said, trying to change the subject. "Must be about three inches by now."

Jim leaned toward Dr. Takamura. "What was she like?" he asked. His hands felt sweaty. Kira was still watching him.

"I didn't really know her that well," the older man said. "She seemed, well, distant somehow. She was always friendly, sometimes very talkative, but she always seemed to be holding something back somehow, never really telling you anything about herself. Paul was always with her. He practically lived at her apartment, and they were thinking of getting one of their own."

The weather seemed to be colder. Kira coughed softly. "Certainly took me back," said Dr. Takamura. "I haven't thought of that whole business in years."

"What happened?" Jim mumbled. "What happened?" he said more clearly.

Dr. Takamura was gazing out at the lawn. "She broke it off. I don't think she ever told him why. Paul was pretty depressed for a while, apathetic about everything, but he pulled together. Jon Aschenbach and I managed to get him through his finals."

Jim shivered. The air was growing cold. "That was a long time ago," said Dr. Takamura.

Ed came out on the porch carrying a tray with three mugs of tea. Jim took one of the mugs and looked on as his brother exchanged greetings with the older man. Ed was the most austere of the clones; he was clean-shaven and wore his hair cropped close to his skull. He spent most of his time on his mathematical studies or his music, and his only close friends were the clones themselves.

Jim heard the voices of the three next to him, but not their words. He saw Paul and Rhoda on the Chicago streets, Paul and Moira. . . . He had thought Moira could not bring herself to accept him because he was a clone. Perhaps it was not that at all, but something else. That should console me, he thought.

No.

This was worse.

I'm living Paul's life, he thought. He felt paralyzed. He saw himself as a puppet walking through an ever-repeating cycle. I'll go through it again, his mind murmured. I'll go on feeling the way I do, acting the way I do, and I won't have any choice. It's all happened before and I have no way of changing it.

Moira was gone. He knew it. Moira was gone from him for good. Rhoda had not come back to Paul. Paul had eventually forgotten Rhoda, and Jim supposed he would forget Moira too. The thought, instead of cheering him, simply sat there in his mind, cold and damp, with no power to move him at all.

The early July weather was still hot. The grass was beginning to look scorched, the flowers were wilted. The sun glared down at the earth, only occasionally disappearing behind a cloud and then emerging once again to mock at the stifled world below. Jim sat on his heels removing weeds that threatened the bushes alongside the house. His hair was tied back on his head. He had debated with himself about shaving his beard, decided against it, knowing he would regret it when winter returned. There was another reason for not shaving it, of course; the beard was his way of differentiating his appearance from that of his brothers.

He put his trowel down, sat back, and looked over at Kira. She was seated under one of the trees reading a book. She held the small microfiche projector to her eyes with one hand, turned a small knob on the projector with the other. Jim still preferred the feel of a book in his hands, enjoyed turning the pages, liked the smell of print and old paper. He had insisted on keeping the books in Paul's library, even though they took up more space than the tiny bits of tape he could have purchased to replace them.

He was like Paul in his attachment to old things. Paul had

remained in his old slightly run-down house in the area surrounding the university while other researchers and professors had moved to living units inside one of the new pyramidal structures only a few minutes away from the campus by train. Paul had remained on earth while many of his colleagues in astrophysics had gone to the moon, had decided he was too old to go. He had raised the clones in the peaceful, almost timeless atmosphere of the university, feeling that this would best prepare them for the complex, almost chaotic world outside. He had wanted them to have a quiet place in which they could discover themselves and gain the intellectual tools that they would need. The universities, so disorganized during Paul's youth, were once again oases of liberal education. Those who had wished for activism had set up their own colleges in the disorderly cities of the continent; and specialists in many fields had their own research centers on ocean floors, in wilderness areas, and on the surfaces of the moon and Mars. The university had been, in a sense, a retreat for the clones, and Jim wondered if they might have become too easily adjusted to it and afraid to look beyond it.

"Why don't you go inside?" he said to Kira. "It's a lot cooler there."

"It's too cool," she replied. "I don't think the regulator's working. I shiver all the time and I had to put blankets on my bed last night."

"I guess I better check it one of these days," Jim said. He wiped sweat off his forehead with the back of his arm. He continued to watch Kira as she resumed reading. She had pinned her hair up on her head and wore a sleeveless blue-green tunic that barely reached the tops of her thighs. To Jim she suggested a woodland sprite who at any moment might disappear among the trees.

In spite of the heat and some painful blisters on his hands, Jim felt content, more at peace than he had been in a long time. He and Kira had been busy since the day Moira had gone home, making repairs on the house, painting the kitchen, putting some new shingles on the roof. He had buried himself in physical work, trying to tire himself so he could sleep soundly, hoping to keep the thought of Moira at a distance, Kira too had time on her hands, as Dr. Takamura had gone to Kenya to aid in training scientists there who wished to clone needed animals for wildlife preserves. He and Kira had worked together, laughing and joking most of the time, exhausting themselves, and one day Jim had realized that his sorrow had receded a little, only returning in force during the night, just before his fatigue pushed him into deep sleep.

Yesterday had been different. They were sitting with Ed on the front porch, talking about one of Jim's poems, listening to Ed play his violin, discussing some of the work Kira had done with Dr. Takamura. They talked for a long time, their minds drawing together, communicating their ideas and feelings with perfect understanding. Then Al and Mike joined them and they sat there until very late, finally giving in reluctantly to sleepiness, and Jim realized as he lay in his bed that he had not thought of Moira all day.

"Hey," he said to Kira, "how about driving up to the lake for a swim? It's too hot to do anything else."

Kira put down her projector. "I'd love to," she said, "but you know there'll be a mob there. I went up with Jonis last month, you could hardly find a place to put a towel down, so we went over to the nude beach and it was worse there. And there were picnickers all over the woods, and empty containers just thrown all around." Kira sighed and pulled up her legs, wrapping her arms around them. "They think the containers'll just disappear, they don't stop to think it takes months for them to dissolve completely. Jonis said she heard that guys go up and take pot shots at the eagles. They don't care—after all, we can always clone more. It makes me so damned mad. I wish they'd kept it closed after reclamation."

We can always clone more. He looked over at Kira and

suddenly felt compassion for the cloned eagles. "We could drive to the park. It's always pretty empty," he said. "It'll be cooler there than here, and we could take some supper for later."

"Great," she said. "At least we'll get away from the house for a while." She stood up, brushed some grass from her tunic, picked up her projector by the handle, and walked toward the house, tanned arms swinging loosely at her sides.

Jim watched her until she disappeared around the corner of the house. She had inherited Paul's gentleness and concern for others. When one of the clones was depressed or worried about something, it was always Kira who was willing to listen or offer moral support. Her creation had been the result of curiosity about how Paul's qualities might manifest themselves in a female. As it happened, she was essentially no different from the brothers, and the concern she expressed for them was probably the product of her studies. She spent as much of her time in seminars discussing ethical problems raised by the biological sciences as in the laboratory. Perhaps she was more mature than he or the others, and there were often times when he thought she was more like Paul than any of them.

He picked up his trowel and followed her inside.

The night air was still warm, but pleasantly so. They had jogged for a while around the perimeter of the park until the heat had subdued them, then had climbed up the hill to the stone wall overlooking the automated highway. They sat on the wall, legs dangling over the side, as they drank beer and finished the remnants of supper.

It had been a pleasant afternoon, but Jim had grown more silent as the sun set. He sat quietly, ignored the highway below, and watched the rising moon. Al had often spoken of going to the moon, joining the people there who were carrying on Paul Swenson's work. Jim tried to concentrate on the lunar disk, tried to ignore the tendrils of thought brushing at the edges of his consciousness. A warm breeze stirred the trees behind him.

He sat with Moira on the wall, held her hand lightly. He gestured toward the moon as he told her of his father's hopes and tried to communicate the reasons behind Paul's dreams. He looked at Moira as she sat listening quietly, seemingly interested, then heard her soft sigh of impatience.

He looked at Kira. She too was watching the rising moon. He wondered what Moira was doing now. He had managed to keep from calling her since she left, afraid that she would misinterpret his motives. He should not have come to the park. It had only deepened his pain, bringing it to the surface once again. Kira turned slightly and her eyes met his.

"I never," he said, "really told you much about Moira, did I? Not even that time . . ." He looked away in embarrassment. *He was standing on the wall, ready to hurl himself toward the brightly lit highway. Kira clung to his arm, silvery tears glistened on her face. "Jump," she shouted, "jump, but you'll have to take me with you."* "Very melodramatic performance," he mumbled, and felt her hand on his arm.

"Don't degrade your pain, Jim," she said softly.

"She didn't just go home for the summer, you know. I don't think she wants to see me when she returns."

"I know," said Kira. "I could tell. You don't have to talk about it, Jim."

"I don't know what's wrong with me," he went on. "It's funny I should care so much about Moira when, if I were honest about it, I'd have to admit I never really knew her. I know she didn't understand me. She never really tried to, she just withdrew." He looked at Kira. "That sounds so cold," he said.

"Don't dwell on it," said Kira softly. "You can't analyze a thing like that, and you'll just feel worse if you try." She swung her legs over the wall and stood up. "Want to take a walk? My legs feel a little stiff."

"Sure." He picked up the small picnic basket and followed her.

They walked along the narrow path that wound through the woods. The path was lighted by the moon, the trees on either side of it seemed to be a dark and impenetrable forest. The smell of pine and wildflowers reached Jim's nostrils. Above him he could hear the movement of a small creature along the limbs of a tree. An owl hooted and was answered by some crickets.

Moira stopped, leaned against one of the trees, and smiled at him. He moved to her side, put his arms around her slender waist, and she rested her head on his shoulder, apparently content.

Jim halted, rested against a tree. His stomach was a closed fist inside him, his face was hot and his mouth dry. He struggled to restrain the moan that threatened to escape his lips. The picnic basket slipped from his fingers and hit the ground with a muffled thud. The handles clattered loudly against the sides of the basket.

"Jim." Kira stood in front of him, clutching his shoulders. "Jim." She released his shoulders and embraced him, cradling his head with one hand. "I know," she said softly.

He was a child again, curled on Paul's lap. "I know," Paul whispered, stroking his hair. "Let it out, Jimmy. Don't ever be ashamed to cry." He squeezed his eyelids together, but the tears would not come. She brushed his hair from his forehead.

She seemed to understand his pain almost instinctively. He rested against her, felt some of the loneliness subside. "I guess," he said finally, "this place must have brought it all back." The tightness of his stomach began to ease.

He stood up straight, arms still around her, and looked into her green eyes, level with his own. She was a dryad, a part of the forest in her tunic and sandaled feet, and it seemed that she might suddenly release him and vanish. He held her more tightly.

He felt his penis stiffen. Startled, he let go of Kira and stood awkwardly in front of her, arms dangling at his sides. She did not move away but continued to stand near him, arms around his shoulders. Her face was pale in the moonlight. She tilted her head to one side. *Don't move away,* her eyes seemed to say. *Don't retreat.* She moved closer to him and kissed his lips gently.

The park had grown silent. He was paralyzed, rooted to the ground as stiffly and surely as the tree he leaned against. He strained to hear the sounds of the forest, could hear only a thundering in his ears.

She released him and they faced each other, silent and still. He tried to raise his arms. They trembled slightly as he reached out to Kira.

She unfastened the sash around her waist, let it flutter to the ground. She grasped her tunic with both hands and pulled it over her head. Then she slipped off her pants, balancing first on one leg, then the other. She moved slowly and as precisely as a dancer; her movements seemed almost stylized. She stood in front of him, and at last she met his eyes again.

He saw apprehension and fear on her face, as well as love and concern. He began to move toward her, taking one step, then a second one—and he was in her arms, holding her tightly. He was afraid to speak. He noticed that Kira too was trembling. He began to stroke her hair.

He loosened his shorts with one hand, dropped them on top of Kira's rumpled tunic. He ran his hands along her smooth back to her buttocks, only slightly wider and rounder than his own. She was no longer trembling.

They knelt and then lay on the ground together. He reached out, held her breasts gently as she watched him. Her face looked like Ed's in the moonlight, ascetic and austere. Then she suddenly smiled, reminding him of Mike in one of his playful moods. She touched his penis, running her thumb lightly over its tip, then grasped him firmly.

His fear receded, and the strength of his longing for her struck him like a wave. She thrust her hips up, pulled him to her. He thought of the uncertainty he had always felt with Moira, the lonely climaxes. There was no uncertainty with Kira. She was his female self, reaching for him now with the same urgency and impatience he felt. Her hand still held him, guided him inside her.

She drew up her knees and they lay on their sides, facing each other. Still gazing into the green eyes identical to his own, he thrust with his hips, ran his hand along her thigh. Her lips parted and he heard a soft sigh. He continued to move and was conscious of her response; she was moaning now, clutching his shoulders tightly. He saw himself as a woman, receiving a man, opening to the hardness that plunged inside her, and knew that she was seeing herself as a man, moving inside the wet and welcoming orifice. They moved together, grinding their hips in perfect rhythm, and he felt the core of his excitement increasing, threatening at any moment to hurl him outside himself for a few timeless seconds.

This has never happened before. He suddenly realized that as he moved inside her, sighing his responses to her moans. *Never before. He saw generation after generation evolve, become more differentiated, genetic structures changing and mutating. He saw millions of men and women seeking mates, trying to find those who would complete them, make them whole again, yet always separated from them by the differences passed on to them by eons of change. He saw Kira and himself, reflections of each other, able to move along their individual paths and yet meet in perfect communication. She was no longer his sister, but his other self, closer to him than a sister could have been, merging with him so completely and perfectly that they were one being.*

He moved with her, sighed with her, was sensitive to every movement of her hands on his body. Then he stopped, held his body absolutely still, prepared himself for the final thrust. She was still also, waited, watched him with wide eyes. Her lips were parted and swollen, the warmth inside her body had grown even more intense.

At last, unable to bear it any longer, he thrust again, and she moved to meet him, gasping quietly at first, then crying out to the night, shattering the silence. He felt himself spurt inside her, and he trembled, moved with her, suspended in a pocket of timelessness. He was adrift with her in a universe contained by the skin of their bodies, and he called out as his pleasure compressed itself in his groin, then erupted throughout his body. He cried out again, could no longer tell which cries were his and which were Kira's. Her green eyes were pools into which he would dive, losing himself forever.

Then it was over and he realized, with a tinge of sadness, how short a time it had actually been. He withdrew from her slowly but remained beside her, resting his head in her arms. He became aware of the sweat that covered their bodies, the warmth of the night. He felt guilt pushing at the edges of his mind, and shame kept his eyes from meeting hers.

Kira, as if responding to his fears, held him more closely. "Don't, Jim," she whispered. "Don't feel ashamed. I love you. I've known it for a while. How could I help it?" She was right, of course, the old codes and ancient prohibitions could not apply to them, had not even allowed for their existence.

He looked at her face. She lay at his side stroking his hair. It was Paul's face that watched him, smiling, gently reassuring him with love. He curled up next to her.

The thunderstorm had departed by morning, leaving behind it cool air and large fluffy clouds. The sun, previously a malevolent eye peering balefully at the earth, was now a friendly presence, occasionally hiding behind one of the white clouds as if ashamed of its former fit of temper. Jim had carried the light plastic chairs off the porch, placed them on top of old newsfax sheets and computer print-outs in the front yard. He aimed his spray can at one, began to cover it with a surface of gray paint.

He glanced at Ed and Kira. They had moved two of the three cars out into the road and were washing them down with the hose. Their shorts and shirts were plastered against their bodies. Kira hooted as she aimed the hose at Ed, drenching him completely. He grabbed the hose from her and began to spray her with water. Kira danced on her toes, laughing loudly.

Jim moved on to the next chair. He had been trying to accept his new relationship with Kira, his feelings for her. He turned it over in his mind, trying to view it objectively: It wasn't harming them, it affected no one else, it gave them pleasure. It seemed cold and somehow negative to think of it that way.

"Is it so strange, Jim?" Kira had said. They were sitting on her bed, legs folded in front of them, elbows on knees, heads in hands, perfectly matched. "It would be stranger if we didn't feel this way, weren't drawn to each other."

He continued to spray the chairs. How do I feel about it? he asked himself. I'm able to reach someone else, able to love and communicate without rejection. He thought of Moira. His love for her had been a nervousness and a feverishness, an uneasiness that was always with him, occupying his entire mind, refusing to let him go. With Kira he was at peace, except for the occasional guilty doubts that nudged him from time to time, then retreated under the onslaught of his rationalizations. With Kira, he could work at his poetry or talk, easily sharing his thoughts and feelings and understanding hers as well.

Kira and Ed were walking toward the house, leaving the hose on the lawn. They seemed to be discussing something. Ed gestured with his right arm as they climbed the steps to the front porch and disappeared into the house. Jim finished spraying the last chair, glared at the hose. All the clones had inherited an almost obsessive tidiness from Paul, and he was annoyed that Ed and Kira had not rewound the hose. It was not like them. I guess they'll do it later, he thought, or maybe they need it for something else.

The chairs would need a little time to dry before he moved them back to the porch. He ambled to the front door, depositing the can on the porch, and went inside.

The house was silent. Al and Mike had gone to the university earlier to do some lab work. Jim wandered through the living room, which was furnished with old overstuffed chairs and sofas. Two learning booths stood in the corner. They resembled large transparent eggs; their screens were blank and their earphones were lying idly on the writing surfaces next to the chairs. Paul had installed two more booths upstairs in the room he had once used as a study. Few people had that many booths in their homes, but Jim knew that few people used the one booth they usually had, preferring to watch the large vidscreens on their walls. Al had left several print-outs on the writing surface of one booth. He was the "pack rat" of the clones and would gather piles of neatly folded print-outs until someone, usually Mike, threw them out. He continued through the living room to the kitchen.

The kitchen was empty. Jim was surprised, having assumed Kira and Ed had come in for a sandwich. He left the kitchen, went back through the living room and up the stairs, decided he would ask them if they wanted help with the hose, ask them if they wanted to have some lunch with him. He walked past Ed's room. The door was open and there was no one inside. He went past Mike's room, then his own, stopped at Kira's door.

It was closed. He knocked, heard the sounds of someone moving in the room. "Kira?" he said. He knocked again, then opened the door.

Kira and Ed were sprawled on the bed, and both were naked. Ed turned and looked at Jim and appeared startled. Kira seemed calm. "Oh, no," said Jim. He clenched his hands into fists, "Oh, no." He was shaking. The twin faces on the bed were watching him.

He wanted to pound his fist into the wall. He turned and fled down the hall to his own room. He stood there, alone, trying to sort out the thoughts that tumbled through his mind. He heard soft footsteps coming down the hall. They stopped at his door. "Jim." He did not move. "Jim." He turned and saw Kira standing in the door, a long red robe draped over her shoulders.

He gestured at the robe. "Your one concession to modesty," he said bitterly. She came into the room and closed the door.

"Why are you so angry, Jim?"

He turned from her and sat on the chair at his desk. "There's no reason to be angry," he muttered. "I found out that we're interchangeable to you too, that's all."

"No, Jim," she said softly, leaning against the door. "That's not what you found out. Do you think for one minute I confuse Ed with you? Forget about yourself for one minute and think about him. He's just about given up trying to reach out to anyone, including us. He's so quiet about his problems, it's easy to pretend he's just shy or not that interested in people. You know how you felt, how lonely you were, but at least you kept trying with Moira, and you could reach me. Ed gave up trying, and about all you've accomplished today is reinforcing the way he feels. Now he's sitting in my room feeling guilty."

Jim looked over at Kira. She was looking at the floor, folding her arms across her chest. "Oh, Jim, I don't know. Maybe I have my own problems too. Don't I have a right to solve them, or at least try? Or am I supposed to limit myself to you, or ignore Ed? Has this business really changed anything you might have found out through me?" She sighed. "Maybe it'll be harder for us, Jim. We have to find our own answers in our own way, and we don't even have the rough guidelines everybody else has. Some people would look at us and talk about incest taboos, and others would probably find it strange if we loved anyone else but the other clones. The point is, we have to try, and maybe we'll make mistakes, but . . ."

She turned and opened the door. "I still love you, Jim, just as much as I did before. Maybe none of us will ever feel the same way about anyone else. Maybe we really can't, being the way we are, and that means that Ed needs me too, and maybe Al and Mike will if they ever look beyond each other."

She left the room but did not close his door. He sat at the desk trying to sort out his thoughts. He considered himself and the other clones, turned over their problems and relationships in his mind, and wondered what he should do now.

He was with Kira, hands on her belly. She looked up at him as he hovered over her, guided his hand between her legs. He felt her wetness with his finger, moved forward and embraced her, embraced himself, and sighed as they merged.

Jim lifted the suitcase and put it in the back seat of the car. Al leaned against the open car door. "We'll miss you," he said to Jim.

"I won't be gone long," he replied. He turned to Kira. Her brow was wrinkled with worry. He reached over to her, grasped her shoulders. "Come on, cheer up," he said. "I'll be back in a month or so. I'm not running away. I know what I'm doing, and I know why."

She smiled at him tentatively, and he kissed her lightly on the forehead. Then he climbed into the car, waved his arm at the porch where Ed and Mike sat.

He had explained himself to them as best he could, and was satisfied that they understood him as well as could be expected. He would drive up to Moira's home first. He would not make demands of her, would not force himself on her. He would not give up if she drew away from him. He would leave and go to a poetry workshop in Minnesota he had heard about, meet people there, be like anyone else.

Kira had come to his room the night before. They lay on his bed, arms and legs entwined, and he told her about his hopes and his plans.

It would be easy to stay with Kira, easy to give up on other people. He would not let himself do it yet, not until he had tried and failed many times.

He started the car and drove away from the house slowly. When he got to the end of the narrow road, he turned his head and saw Kira and Al walking to the front porch. Suddenly he felt doubtful about his actions, wondered if he should leave, asked himself if he really wanted to go.

He continued to drive until the house was out of sight and he was on the road leading to the automated highway. He thought of Kira again, saw her head resting on his shoulder, and wondered if he were making a mistake. Will anyone love me the way you do? he asked. Will I love anyone else as completely? The image of Kira faded from his mind. She had given him as many questions as answers.

The world out there was just as worthy of his attention as his own personal problems. It was a world very different from the sheltered enclave of the university, a world of neatly organized cities under pyramids and domes, and disorganized cities that sprawled across the landscape. It was a world of people who looked beyond the earth to the stars, and people who sought to preserve old customs and ancient ways. It was a world of abundance for many and starvation for some, of green and fertile reclaimed wildernesses and eroded deserts. It was time that he tried to understand his own place in this world.

He drove the car onto the bypass, punched out his destination, and leaned back as the highway control took over, guided his car around the curved bypass, and shot him forward into the stream of cars on the highway.

RON GOULART

Whistler

His agent appeared on the pixphone screen and asked him, "Do you have any good wallpaper ideas?"

Mel Felson was at his drawing board, tilted far to the left. He was a dark-haired moderate-sized man of twenty-nine, wearing a green all-purpose suit. He gave the phone on his taboret a quick side glance. "What now?" he asked and went back to watching his colonial-style dome house, which lay a half acre from his domed studio.

"Can you draw in a position like that?" asked Bubber Krigstein. As usual he was sitting surrounded by water-filled cushions in his plain-walled Manhattan office.

"No," answered Felson. Sanitized smoke was coming up out of the pseudometal chimney atop his house, corkscrewing away in the clear spring afternoon. "Excuse me a second, Bubber." He put his agent on hold, punched the living-room phone button.

"Hello," answered Whistler in his deepest voice. The oval

phone screen stayed dark. Somewhere in the unseen living room a middle-aged woman was laughing. "Felson residence."

"What are you doing with the fireplace, nitwit?" Felson asked the blacked-out Whistler. "It's the middle of May."

"Nostalgia knows no season, my boy," replied Whistler. "Nor love, I might add."

"What are you burning over there?"

"We're toasting marshmallows," said Whistler in his low vibrant voice. "Sometimes in the hurlyburly of everyday life, Mel, we forget the little simple—"

"Okay, okay." He punched Whistler off, his small frail agent back on.

As usual Bubber was hunkered under his broad metal desk, walled with water-filled cushions. He was trying on tough-plastic helmets. "Your fortune is made," he said when he noticed Felson was back.

"Bubber, it's 1991," Felson told his agent. "We've had nearly a half century of relative peace. There's not going to be another big war."

"There's the insidious thing about a sneak attack," said Bubber. "The unexpectedness of the thing." He selected a lime-green crash helmet. "Listen, your money problem is over."

"Which money problem? The alimony to Rosa, the mortgage and property tax payments, the annual assessment from the political party of my choice, the—"

"All of them," cut in Bubber. "An artist with your talent, Mel, you should be making more than a mere thirty thousand a year."

"If I had an agent who wasn't always scrunched up under his desk anticipating Armageddon, I might." Felson looked away from Bubber. The safe smoke was still spinning up. "Okay, what have you got, a good illustration job?"

"Better than illustration, Mel." The frail Bubber smiled. "What do you know about the humorous wallpaper field?"

"Nothing." Felson suddenly left his drawing board and dashed to the studio's view window. The house door leading to the patio ramp had popped open. A plump woman wearing only a suit of one-piece all-season underwear was dancing down the ramp scattering artificial flowers. "Wait a minute, Bubber." Felson started to hit the living-room button, then hesitated. More slowly he returned to the window. "Bubber," he said back at the phone, "has the check from the Gow Patriotic License Plate Company come in yet?"

"Any day now, they promise. The only guy who can sign checks had to teleport to Ecuador to fit some patriotic plates on a fleet of armored tanks. Why?"

"Mrs. Gow is out dancing naked on my lawn and I'd feel better if it was too late for Gow to stop the money." He punched the living-room phone button. "Nitwit," he said when Whistler, bare-chested and grinning, appeared on the phone screen. "You didn't tell me you were roasting marshmallows with the wife of one of my clients."

"A gentleman, my boy, doesn't blurt out every detail of his affairs." Whistler was tall, handsome, mustached, tan.

"Look, you nitwit gadget, you screw me up once more and, I don't give a damn, it's going to be down in Nardikian's basement for you," warned Felson. "How did you meet Mrs. Gow anyway?"

"She came by asking after you one afternoon while you were over visiting your fiancée in Westport," said Whistler, smoothing his auburn mustache. "I think, if the truth were told, she'd hoped to find you alone. She claimed to be delivering some license plate proofs. Bulky things, aren't they? Something to do with famous generals who seem to salute as you pass on the road or in the air. I put them aside for you someplace or other, my boy. A novel idea, but then I've always told you—"

"Why is she dancing on my lawn?" The plump Mrs. Gow had left the patio ramp and was ankle deep in plaskolite grass.

"She's feeling uninhibited," explained Whistler. "Haven't you ever felt that way when you and your fiancée—"

"Not in the middle of the afternoon, in broad daylight, out on the lawn, no," Felson told Whistler. "Throw a blanket over her and drag her back inside. Gow lives right here in Brimstone, Connecticut, you know. Suppose he happens to fly over this neighborhood in his hopper and looks down and sees his nitwit fat wife being uninhibited on my lawn. It would be the end of any more patriotic license plate work for me."

"An artist with your potential, my boy, shouldn't—"

"Get her inside now," ordered Felson. He punched back his agent, turned away from the window.

"Why is she dancing on your lawn?" asked Bubber. "Do you know her?"

"We have mutual friends," said Felson. "What's this about funny wallpaper?"

The frail agent reached up into his crash helmet for a memo. "Can you teleport to Youngstown, Ohio, this afternoon and see the vice president of the ReSyk Paper Company?"

"No."

"Sure you can. They're paying a thousand dollars per roll."

"What kind of payment is that?"

"Per roll of humorous wallpaper. It takes—let's see where I scribbled that figure down—it takes twelve humorous drawings and captions per roll, this guy Norge Heaslip out there in Youngstown tells me. He can use six rolls by you. Okay, say it takes you a week to do a roll. That's six big ones in as many weeks, less my twenty per cent."

"I don't know anything about wallpaper."

"You've seen it on walls, haven't you?"

"Well, yes."

"So this guy Heaslip noticed some of those humorous bedsheets you did and he likes your work. Go see him."

"Wait. Norge Heaslip lives right over in New Canaan. Can't I talk to him at home?"

"He tells me he leaves his work at the office and teleports to the suburbs to relax. He prefers to talk business in Ohio," explained Bubber. "You might take some of those bedsheets with you."

"They're all rumpled."

"Don't you keep a clean set of sheets and pillow cases in your portfolio?"

"I did, but you don't know what an android thinks is funny."

"Huh?"

"Never mind. Give me Heaslip's address out there in Ohio and the number of the nearest teleport station," said Felson. "I've got a date with Jalna tonight, you know."

"Heaslip is a man of action. He shouldn't take more than an hour or two."

Felson walked away from the phone. He'd turned toward the window again. Mrs. Gow was no longer in sight. But a man with a crinkled face was peering over the high ornamental hedge to the left of Felson's dome house.

When he became aware of Felson's gaze, he ducked away and was gone.

"I put Heaslip's address in another one of these protective hats," Bubber was saying. "Be patient."

Felson, frowning, returned to his drawing board. He picked up an electric pencil. If he could make an extra $6,000 or so out of this wallpaper job, even though it wasn't the kind of thing he wanted to do, then he'd be that much closer to being able to get out of debt and married again. All this stuff made sense if Jalna was at the end of it someplace. His agent gave him the address and he jotted it down on the edge of a rough sketch of a nondenominational wedding cake he was designing. "Okay, Bubber. I'll get my samples together, jump in the hopper, and fly over to the Brimstone teleport station. I'll let you know what happens."

"I sense this is the next step up for you, Mel," said Bubber from under his desk. "Remember, you can't always do what you want and expect to rise to the heights."

"Okay, I'll try it your way." Felson turned off things in his studio, gathered up a portfolio of samples, and went outside to the two-deck landcar and air hopper port. His hopper was just rising up into the warm blue afternoon.

"Taking the fair Mrs. Gow for a little joyride, my boy," announced Whistler over the cockpit mike.

Mrs. Gow was laughing again and she was still in her all-season underwear.

Felson watched his egg-colored hopper climb away until it banked toward Westport. He got into his landcar, clicked on the electric motor. "Nardikian is going to have to work on that nitwit mechanism again," he said.

Twenty-five minutes later he was in Ohio.

Felson had acquired Whistler five weeks earlier. As his friend Nardikian had explained it, they would make maybe $10,000 a year each with Whistler once Nardikian worked everything out.

Nardikian had appeared after dark on a rainy April night, with Whistler in an opaque plyosak. "I'd keep him at my house, Mel, except Magda doesn't think it'd be so good around the boys," Nardikian explained, dabbing raindrops off his contact lenses. He was thirty-four and overweight, darker than Felson and shaggier.

"Keep who?"

"Let me bring him inside."

Felson stepped aside as Nardikian and the six-foot-tall sack walked into his dome house. "What is it in there?"

"You're alone? Jalna didn't drop in after I called you?"

"No, she's out marching on the Telepoverty Agency in Stamford." Felson noticed whatever it was in the sack was wearing very handsome Swiss shoes. "Is that a guy in there?"

"Sit on the sofa, Whistler," ordered Nardikian.

The tall sack strode across the living room to seat itself on the air column sofa.

"Is your friend a celebrity who doesn't want to be recognized?"

Shrugging out of his rain poncho and letting the robot arm in the wall closet take it, Nardikian said, "You live alone for the most part."

"Since Rosa got the quick Guanajuato divorce and teleported to Holland to live with that support hose salesman," admitted Felson. "But Jalna's here now and then. We're engaged, you know."

"Congratulations," said the shaggy Nardikian. "First off, this thing is not exactly stolen. So you won't have to worry really about the legal angle. What the situation is, I have an informal option. Admittedly the option is with the night watchman, but I think it'll hold up. They're going to collapse anyway. And once I get the details worked out, it's $20,000 a year for us, split down the middle."

Felson signaled the robot bar. When it rolled across the living room to him, he dialed a soyale for Nardikian and a vitamin C screwdriver for himself. "Who've you got in that nitwit sack?"

Coming into the room to take his glass of ale, Nardikian said, "That is a first class screwing machine you see before you."

Felson glanced again at the expensive Swiss shoes. "You swiped an android?"

"I optioned it," corrected his friend.

"From where?"

"Whistler is from the Famous Doctors Sex Research Foundation in Westport," Nardikian said. "His full designation is Whistler-260/OR-fb87."

"The FDSRF?"

"Yes, from their Orgasm Wing."

"I heard, because they're no longer getting government money, they were about to fold."

"Exactly." Nardikian grinned. "The Orgasm Wing has been idle for three months already. Poor Whistler was gathering dust in the clinic warehouse. See, the nephew of the night watchman there works with me at Technokraft. He told me Famous Doctors had fallen on bad days and had something like two dozen or more sex research androids simply sitting around unused."

"Why'd you pick this one?"

"Ah." Nardikian crossed the thermal rug to the shrouded android, then tugged at the sacking. "Lift your ass a sec, Whistler." He gathered the plyosak completely off. "I picked the best-looking one."

"Good evening," said Whistler in a deep pleasant voice. "A privilege to meet you, my boy." He had the appearance of a very handsome man in his late thirties. Even after being walked around in a sack, his auburn hair, flecked with gray, was unrumpled.

"He's got what they list in the catalogue as a classic profile." Nardikian touched at a silver disk behind the android's left ear. "Turn so Mel can see the side view."

"Glad to oblige, my boy."

"Okay," said Felson. "He's cute head-on and sideways. What do you plan to do with him?"

"What do *we* plan to do," said Nardikian. "I'm going to share this all with you, fifty-fifty." He shook his head, sighing. "A guy with your talent, who can draw like you, shouldn't be getting by on thirty thousand a year. I want to see you pulling in fifty thou at the very least, Mel. Then you can get out of hock and marry Jalna. Jalna is very right for you, and I doubt she'll ever run off to Holland with a sock salesman who—"

"How are we going to use a sex research robot to make ourselves an extra twenty thousand each year?"

"Tell him what you did at the clinic," Nardikian told the android.

"Wooed the ladies."

"He's programmed to be polite in formal social occasions," said Nardikian. "Actually, this guy was built especially for the Orgasm Wing. He's guaranteed to produce a climax in eighty-seven per cent of the cases."

"Ninety-one per cent according to the last print-out on the orgasm computer," corrected Whistler.

Nardikian watched the android with narrowed eyes for a few seconds. "Ninety-one per cent," he said. "Not only that, he's got every lady-pleasing trait and mannerism built into him. Women see him, listen to that voice, jump in the sack and *bam!*"

"In at least ninety-one per cent of the encounters," said Whistler. "I also have a technicolor camera built into my male member."

"That's an extra," said Nardikian. "Though maybe some of the ladies would care for such photos."

"Also," added Whistler, "when I fondle the subject I can get an instant electrocardiogram reading."

"I'll do the rest of the explaining," said Nardikian.

"Oh, certainly. Forgive me for stepping out of line, my boy."

To Felson, Nardikian continued: "The little silver knick-knack behind his ear is an addition of my own. It's a parasite gimmick which gives us extra control over him. I'll show you how to work it before I leave."

"I can play stereophonic music out my ears." Whistler smiled.

"Wait, Nardikian. You want to leave this guy here?"

His shaggy friend said, "I can't keep him around our place, Mel. An android designed to screw broads, snap pictures inside their private parts while playing mood music out his ears—it's not a good example for the boys to have around."

Felson, while dialing another vitamin C screwdriver, said, "I still don't understand how we make money off him."

"We lease him."

"Lease him. To who?"

"Ladies," said Nardikian. "Lonely ladies. Look around you. Observe the social patterns of Brimstone, Wilton, Westport, etcetera. You're surrounded by lonely broads whose husbands are continually and eternally teleporting to the four corners of the earth, and occasionally to the moon, on business. Why, on any given night I'd guess forty per cent of the women in Brimstone and environs are lonely."

"Fifty-two per cent actually," offered Whistler.

"Okay, Fifty-two per cent," said Nardikian. "You know, Mel, I hear a couple of the bigger android outfits are already fooling with the idea of manufacturing mechanical companions for women. What we have is a chance to pioneer."

"Oh, so?" said Felson. "Here I am, a commercial artist with what everybody agrees is great potential and I'm making a living drawing montages of famous generals for patriotic license plates and designing decorative bunny rabbit motifs for disposable diapers and coming up with gags for humorous pictorial bedsheets and matching pillowcases—and now you want me to become a pimp."

"Could I face my boys if I thought of this venture as nothing more than us becoming hustlers?" asked Nardikian. "Nobody wants a pimp for a father. But a father making an extra ten thousand a year is something else altogether."

"How do we sell him to people, on street corners?"

"I haven't yet worked out all the details," admitted Nardikian. "And I want to run a few tests on him, maybe make a few adaptations."

"I'm perfect now," Whistler pointed out, smiling.

"You're sure that parasite of yours controls him?"

"Sure," Nardikian assured Felson. "You don't want to control him too much or he loses his spontaneity and charm. Lonely broads don't want to shack up with a dull clunk."

"I doubt they want to shack up with a gadget at all," said Felson as he finished his second drink.

"On the contrary, my boy."

"If we merchandise this properly," said Nardikian, "it'll work. I admit I had to acquire Whistler a few weeks earlier than I planned because of the watchman's fouled-up vacation schedule, but I guarantee you I'll have the whole operation worked out by the end of the month." He put a hand on Felson's shoulder. "I've got him rigged to be docile. He doesn't require food or oiling or anything. He'll sit quietly in one of your spare rooms until we're ready to cash in."

"I don't know if I want to cash in on some nitwit andy with a camera in his pecker."

Patting Felson's shoulder, Nardikian said, "Even if you decide not to come in, Mel, even if you decide to pass up that extra ten thousand or more per year . . . do me a favor and keep the thing here at your place. Magda simply won't let me have him in the house. A favor?"

Finally Felson said, "Okay, I'll try it your way."

"I know my stay here will be a mutually satisfying one." Whistler got up, walked to the robot bar, and dialed himself a pseudomartini. "I've been programmed to drink on pleasant social occasions," he said. "Cheers."

"Sure, cheers." Felson went over to the living-room porthole and watched the spring rain spatter it.

Felson came home from Youngstown, Ohio, with a contract for six rolls of humorous wallpaper plus an option on a dozen more. It was twilight when he drove into the lower level of the car port. His hopper was back on the top deck.

Whistler was back too. The handsome android was reclining on the imitation bear rug in front of the white metal fireplace, wearing a one-piece nearsilk lounging suit. "Your portfolio looks awfully lumpy, my boy."

"It's full of wallpaper samples. Now, Whistler—"

"Jalna will be a half hour late."

"She called?"

"Obviously, my boy. A stunning girl, let me say once again, though a little slender for my tastes. She phoned only a few moments ago to say she's going to be tied up at the Rebuild Brazil rally longer than she anticipated. Something about the guest speaker having to wait for the effects of the police docility gas to—"

"Okay, fine." Felson flung his portfolio on the sofa and a roll of wallpaper unfurled out of it. The roll was covered with drawings of people with sausagelike noses. "You're not to borrow my hopper any more."

"It was a spur of the moment thing, my boy. I apologize for Mrs. Gow and myself."

"What happened to the idea you were supposed to sit contentedly in my guest room until Nardikian works out his nitwit get-rich-quick scheme?"

"A man gets restless after a month."

"A month? Two days after I took you in you were sneaking off, haunting out-of-the-way cocktail bars, crashing riding club dances, then hitting Seventies Nostalgia Rock Concerts and picking up middle-aged broads and bringing them home. I've had to keep my own fiancée out of here because I never know what I'm going to walk in on. Restless?"

"I was programmed to be horny, my boy, if I may so phrase it."

"Nardikian swears, every time I can reach him on the pixphone, that the gimmick he attached to you is sufficient to control you. But it doesn't work for me."

The handsome android said, "Nardikian was so engrossed in his own work he probably didn't put his best effort into the parasite control device. And now he's even more immersed in work."

"Yeah, I hadn't anticipated, nor had he, his having to teleport off to Tuzla, Yugoslavia, for Technokraft the week after he dumped you on me." Felson loosened his collar seam. "Anyway, I still want you to stay right around home. And now I have to take a shower."

"Better wait until Mrs. Sven-Elven is finished, my boy."

"Mrs. Sven-Elven?"

"She dropped by for an after ski drink," explained Whistler. "She's just teleported back from the Alps somewhere. One thing led to another, as it does in ninety-one per cent of the cases."

"Christ," said Felson. "You've got the wife of Dr. Cosmo Sven-Elven, the head of the Famous Doctors Sex Research Foundation of Westport, you've got her dropping in on you on her way home from the Alps?"

"Yes, my boy. Those are her skis leaning over against your —"

"The head of the nitwit clinic you're a fugitive from, his wife is in my shower alcove? Hasn't she recognized you as a runaway mechanism?"

"Not as yet, my boy. The lady takes very little interest in the doctor's work. She explained that to me when I met her at a hunt ball last week," said Whistler. "By the way, I'm not a runaway. I was borrowed."

"Maybe you ought to be returned to FDSRF."

"That would mean no chance of big money for you," reminded Whistler. "Besides I don't think such a life style would suit me any longer."

Felson inhaled more air than he needed. "I'll go out without a shower." He turned and left his house.

Jalna McKeefer was a willowy brunette of twenty-seven, lovely and intense. "Open it," she suggested.

Felson put his hopper into an automatic circling pattern over the dark Long Island Sound. "You shouldn't buy me presents all the time, Jalna."

"If you love someone, you give them things." The lovely girl loosened her seat straps so she could speak closer to his right ear. "Besides I got it practically free for joining the Doubleday Gadget Club."

When Felson opened the small carton Jalna'd dropped in his lap he found a silver hand inside. "A paper weight?"

"No, push the red button on the wrist."

Felson did that. The silver hand crawled out of its plastic excelsior, skittered across his thigh, settled in his crotch, and grabbed for his fly. Felson caught the hand up, pushed the red button again. He tilted the gadget so he could read the tiny printing in its palm. " 'Wakzoff, a product of New Rio.' " Felson held the hand by its thumb at arm's length. "You mean this is a gadget to help people masturbate?"

"It sounded sort of fascinating."

Holding the gift box at arm's length, Felson dropped the silver hand into it. "Jalna, I don't need any more sex gadgets. Not with—" He stopped.

"Not with what?"

Tossing the hand box into the back seat of the night-circling hopper, he said, "Jalna, you know the guy who's my . . . my house guest?"

"Whistler, of course. He's quite attractive, in a formal sort of way. Though he doesn't have your knobby animal pull." She kissed his temple.

Felson said, "He's an android."

The pretty brunette leaned away from him, hugging herself. "An android?"

"Yeah, he was designed to . . . for the purpose of having . . . you know, with women."

"Mel, you mean you've got hold of one of those fornicating andies similar to the ones they use at the Famous Doctors Sex Research Foundation of Westport? Why, that's fascinating."

"Not similar. Whistler *is* one of the FDSRF machines." He watched the dark water and the shore lights on both sides of the Sound. Felson explained about Whistler and about Nardikian's moneymaking idea, about all the troubles the android had brought down on him.

Jalna hugged Felson. "That's wonderful of you, Mel. Taking risks, planning enterprises. I told you you had terrific potential," she said while kissing him on the face and ear. "You're going to get out of the financial hole sooner than you think. I can quit my job as associate professor of animated cartooning at Konnecticut Kollege and we can marry. You know how I feel about marriage."

"I feel that way too, Jalna, anxious."

She nudged him in the side. "I mean how I feel about the relative position of the male and female in the marriage relationship."

Felson glanced over into the back seat. He thought he'd

heard the silver fingers drumming impatiently on the side of the carton. "Yes, you believe in a return to the simple marriage patterns of the early part of the century. Man in charge, woman subservient. Well, I think I'm the type who can take charge of things."

"Haven't I always told you so?" She leaned against him, rubbing at his chest and stomach.

Felson closed his eyes, smiling. Then suddenly sat up shouting, "Yow! The hand's loose."

"That's me, Mel."

"Oh, yes, sorry." He grinned at her, nodding. "All the nitwit things I do now, the patriotic license plates, the pillowcases, the humorous wallpaper—"

"I didn't know you were doing wallpaper."

"The job just came in. I'll tell you about it later. All this nitwit stuff I do, it makes sense because of you, Jalna."

"Of course, Mel." She kissed him once again.

During the next two weeks Felson didn't see as much of Jalna. The number of Rebuild Brazil demonstrations and Telepoverty marches seemed to increase. With Jalna's already heavy teaching schedule at Konnecticut Kollege, there was little time left for them. Felson minded, but he was busy with roughing out funny wallpaper ideas.

Gow didn't give him any new patriotic license plate work. Felson suspected the plate manufacturer had found out about Whistler and Mrs. Gow, but his frail agent insisted Gow's only objection was that Felson's General Patton had turned out too amiable. Bubber Krigstein came up with a new job, doing storyboards for a hand puppet newscast on the National Kids Network, which made up for the Gow loss.

Midday on a clear blue Wednesday at the end of May a chubby man in a powdered wig phoned Felson. "Mr. Felson, this is the Old Original Yankee Tavern and Inn."

"I haven't heard of you."

"We only opened last month. We're on the Boston Post

Road near Westport." He adjusted his colonial wig. "The reason I'm calling, Mr. Felson, is I can't seem to find a listing for Mr. Whistler. The phone people tell me you're the person listed at the address he aways gives."

Felson asked, "Whistler owes you money?"

"I'm sure it's slipped his mind The room fees we can carry for a while. However, the two cases of imported California Fortified Pineapple Wine I had to pay for out of my own pocket. I don't like to burst in on him when he's here with one of his ladies, so I'm making this discreet call to you."

Felson looked out his studio window in time to see his hopper, with Whistler at the controls, rise up and away. "Okay, I'll give you my bank computer number and you can charge Mr. Whistler's bill to me. How much?"

"The wine comes to two hundred and forty dollars," said the Old Original Yankee Tavern and Inn accountant. "That includes corkage fees."

"Okay, my bank number is 206-9MF602. Goodbye." Felson was going to put in an overseas call to Nardikian, who was in Kano, Nigeria, all this week, when the phone buzzed again.

This time a vaguely familiar wrinkle-faced man was on the oval screen. He was sobbing softly. "I've done a terrible thing."

This sounded like a crank call, except Felson thought he'd seen this particular crank before. "Beg pardon?"

"What possessed me to do it?" sighed the small wrinkled man. "Perhaps jealousy mingled with blind rage. We must not rule out the deep love and long-term affection extending over nearly twelve, so I thought until recently, happy years of domestic harmony. The whole phenomenon of the fit of passion is one we have hardly studied sufficiently. As I was planning to tell my gathered colleagues here in Yawata, Japan, we have only—"

"You wouldn't be Dr. Cosmo Sven-Elven, would you?"

The small man paused in his sobbing to nod and attempt a grin. "Yes, I am. I'm here in Yawata attending a symposium on transistorized fellation. I'm the keynote speaker, otherwise I'd teleport right back there to Brimstone, Connecticut, now. As it is, I left my colleagues dangling in mid-aphorism to rush out and call you. What impels us to act on impulses such as these? It is a topic fraught with—"

"Why did you want to call me?"

"I'm feeling regret over the terrible irrational thing I've done."

"You're the guy who's been peeping over my hedges," said Felson, realizing where he'd seen this wrinkled man before.

"Also looking down your chimney and bugging your bedchambers," said the sniffling doctor. "Actually I've been keeping tabs not on you but on my strayed android and my—"

"You can have Whistler back if that's what's bothering you. So stop crying."

"No, I'm not crying over that," said Dr. Sven-Elven. "Nor am I crying over the infidelity of my wife, Mrs. Sven-Elven, and my inability to face her and tell her she was actually carrying on with one of my own inventions. Let me make it clear what it is I have done. Perhaps a more rational man would not have followed such a course, but I was far from rational this morning before I teleported for Japan."

"What exactly did—"

"I planted a bomb inside Whistler."

"A bomb?"

"When it goes off it will demolish him and Mrs. Sven-Elven."

"A bomb?"

"Isn't that a foolish thing to have done? A man in my position, head of the Famous Doctors Sex Research Foundation of Westport. A man of whom *Who's Who in the East* has —"

"Get back to the bomb, Doctor."

"I slipped into your house at dawn this morning. While you slept I installed a small powerful bomb of my own design into Whistler's interior workings."

"How'd he sit still for that?"

"I know how to control him after all. I installed my little bomb and thereafter wiped all memory of my visit from his brain."

"When's this bomb set to go off?"

The small wrinkled doctor sobbed once more. "That's where I was insidiously clever. You can't imagine how blind rage inspires a man. The bomb is so linked with Whistler's inner mechanisms that it will explode the next time he has sexual intercourse," he said. "From things my wife said and hinted last evening I know she's having another meeting with him this afternoon."

"Oy," said Felson.

"My sentiments exactly. I was hardly beyond the opening paragraphs of my address when my head cleared and I realized what an awful thing I had done. Admittedly the device itself is a clever one and—"

"Can I turn the bomb off?"

"A very perceptive question, Mr. Felson. I've called you in the hope you'll be able to do exactly that. Can you draw well enough to copy a simple diagram I'm going to show you?"

"Yes." Felson picked up an electric pencil, then copied the drawing Dr. Sven-Elven was holding up on the phone screen. As he drew he made notes on what the doctor was saying about the bomb and how to deactivate it.

"Go on over to your house right now and do it," said Dr. Sven-Elven when Felson was finished. "I'll stay on the line in case you want to consult me further."

"Whistler left here twenty minutes ago," said Felson. "I don't know where he was going."

"That complicates our problem," said the doctor.

Felson leaped from his landcar while the white-wigged lot attendant still had his hand on the door handle. Mrs. Sven-Elven had not been at home. Her door-answering robot had said she'd gone to a Pro Telepoverty rally. Felson hadn't bothered to check the rally out. Whistler would never meet her at something like that.

Felson went sprinting along the outdoor gallery of past presidents of the United States. The Abraham Lincoln android tipped his stovepipe hat to him. In the registration office he encountered only a computerized sign-in desk. Ending his run against the low wide desk, Felson thumped on its top with his knuckles. "Do you have a Mr. Whistler registered here?" From what the accountant had said this morning, this inn had become one of Whistler's favorite rendezvous spots.

"We cannot give out information about our guests," said the desk.

Felson pounded on the desk top again harder. "Do you have somebody human I can talk to? This is really important."

The desk made an odd grating noise. "Whistler, Mr. and Mrs., Cottage Twenty-six," it blurted. "Oops. I wasn't supposed to tell you that, sir. You jiggled me with your last brutal thump. Please ignore what—"

Felson spun, ran from the office. Stretching away from the big pseudocolonial main building of the inn was a scatter of some three dozen small Old English style cottages surrounded by newly planted elms and white birches. Felson, at a fast jog, headed for the cottages.

Cottage Twenty-six wasn't next to Cottage Twenty-five. Catching his breath, Felson looked around him. "There it is," he said. The cottage sat off by itself beyond an artificial brook. Grabbing the bomb-dismantling drawing out of his pocket, Felson trotted around the pool.

He ran up the nearstone steps, hitting the cottage's door with his shoulder and catching the knob as he did. The door wasn't locked. It swung in with him pressed against it.

"Don't make another move," he shouted.

Whistler, naked to the waist, was standing with one knee on the edge of a spool bed across the room. His left hand was on the seam of his trousers. "Mel, my boy," he said. "I can explain everything to you."

"You and Mrs. Sven—" Felson blinked. It wasn't Mrs. Sven-Elven sitting up in the bed.

"I hope you didn't come here with the idea of shooting someone," said the willowy Jalna. Reaching beneath her, she tugged part of a blue sheet loose, wrapped it around her bare shoulders. "Because it is still you I'm most fond of, Mel. The thing is, I found myself getting more and more fascinated by Whistler. After you'd confided in me he was an android. I think it's perfectly natural to experiment some before marriage."

Felson glanced from his fiancée to the android, not speaking.

"I don't know what sort of scene you had in mind, my boy, when you came charging in here like some turn-of-the-century swain. Let me assure you, as the lovely Jalna has, that this is nothing serious."

Jalna said, "I'm sorry to see you reacting this way, Mel. We all have to learn to live with things as we go through life. I think if you left now, somewhat more quietly than you arrived, things will work out."

Whistler smiled, nodding. "That would be the wise thing to do, my boy."

After a few seconds Felson said, "Okay, I'll try it your way."

He walked out of the cottage, closing the door gently behind him. When he was beside the decorative pond again, he folded up the bomb drawing, tore it in quarters, and dropped the pieces toward the still water.

ROBERT SILVERBERG

In the Group

It was a restless time for Murray. He spent the morning sand-trawling on the beach at Acapulco. When it began to seem like lunchtime he popped to Nairobi for mutton curry at the Three Bells. It wasn't lunchtime in Nairobi, but these days any restaurant worth eating at stayed open round the clock. In late afternoon, subjectivewise, he paused for pastis and water in Marseilles, and toward psychological twilight he buzzed back home to California. His inner clock was set to Pacific Time, so reality corresponded to mood: night was falling, San Francisco glittered like a mound of jewels across the bay. He was going to do Group tonight. He got Kay on the screen and said, "Come down to my place tonight, yes?"

"What for?"

"What else? Group."

She lay in a dewy bower of young redwoods, three hundred miles up the coast from him. Torrents of unbound milk-white hair cascaded over her slender bare honeycolored body. A multicarat glitterstone sparkled fraudulently between her flawless little breasts. Looking at her, he felt his hands tightening into desperate fists, his nails ravaging his palms. He loved her beyond all measure. The intensity of his love overwhelmed and embarrassed him.

"You want to do Group together tonight?" she asked. "You and me?" She didn't sound pleased.

"Why not? Closeness is more fun than apartness."

"Nobody's ever apart in Group. What does mere you-and-me physical proximity matter? It's irrelevant. It's obsolete."

"I miss you."

"You're with me right now," she pointed out.

"I want to touch you. I want to inhale you. I want to taste you."

"Punch for tactile then. Punch for olfactory. Punch for any input you think you want."

"I've got all sensory channels open already," Murray said. "I'm flooded with delicious input. It still isn't the same thing. It isn't enough, Kay."

She rose and walked slowly toward the ocean. His eyes tracked her across the screen. He heard the pounding of the surf.

"I want you right beside me when Group starts tonight," he told her. "Look, if you don't feel like coming here, I'll go to your place."

"You're being boringly persistent."

He winced. "I can't help it. I like being close to you."

"'You have a lot of old-fashioned attitudes, Murray." Her voice was so cool. "Are you aware of that?"

"I'm aware that my emotional drives are very strong. That's all. Is that such a sin?" Careful, Murray. A serious error in tactics just then. This whole conversation a huge mistake, most likely. He was running big risks with her by pushing too hard, letting too much of his crazy romanticism reveal itself so early. His obsession with her, his impossible new possessiveness, his weird ego-driven exclusivism. His love. *Yes:* his love. She was absolutely right, of course. He was basically old-fashioned. Wallowing in emotional atavism. You-and-me stuff. I, me, me, mine. This unwillingness to share her fully in Group. As though he had some special claim. He was pure nineteenth century underneath it all. He had only just discovered that, and it had come as a surprise to him. His sick archaic fantasies aside, there was no reason for the two of them to be side by side in the same room during Group, not unless they were the ones who were screwing, and the copulation schedule showed Nate and Serena on tonight's ticket. Drop it, Murray. But he couldn't drop it. He said into her stony silence, "All right, but at least let me set up an inner intersex connection for you and me. So I can feel what you're feeling when Nate and Serena get it on."

"Why this frantic need to reach inside my head?" she asked.

"I love you."

"Of course you do. We all love all of Us. But still, when you try to relate to me one-on-one like this, you injure Group."

"No inner connection, then?"

"No."

"Do you love me?"

A sigh. "I love Us, Murray."

That was likely to be the best he'd get from her this evening. All right. All right. He'd settle for that, if he had to. A crumb here, a crumb there. She smiled, blew him an amiable kiss, broke the contact. He stared moodily at the dead screen. All right. Time to get ready for Group. He turned to the lifesize screen on the east wall and keyed in the visuals for preliminary alignment. Right now Group Central was sending its test pattern, stills of all of tonight's couples. Nate and Serena were in the center, haloed by the glowing nimbus that marked them as this evening's performers. Around the periphery Murray saw images of himself, Kay, Van, JoJo,

Nikki, Dirk, Conrad, Finn, Lanelle, and Maria. Bruce, Klaus, Mindy, and Lois weren't there. Too busy, maybe. Or too tired. Or perhaps they were in the grip of negative unGroup-like vibes just at the moment. You didn't have to do Group every night if you didn't feel into it. Murray averaged four nights a week. Only the real bulls, like Dirk and Nate, routinely hit seven out of seven. Also JoJo, Lanelle, Nikki—the Very Hot Ladies, he liked to call them.

He opened up the audio. "This is Murray," he announced. "I'm starting to synchronize."

Group Central gave him a sweet unwavering A for calibration. He turned his receiver to match the note. "You're at 432," Group Central said. "Bring your pitch up a little. There. There. Steady. 440, fine." The tones locked perfectly. He was synched in for sound. A little fine tuning on the visuals next. The test pattern vanished and the screen showed only Nate, naked, a big cocky rockjawed man with a thick mat of curly black hair covering him from thighs to throat. He grinned, bowed, preened. Murray made adjustments until it was all but impossible to distinguish the three-dimensional holographic projection of Nate from the actual Nate, hundreds of miles away in his San Diego bedroom. Murray was fastidious about these adjustments. Any perceptible drop-off in reality approximation dampened the pleasure Group gave him. For some moments he watched Nate striding bouncily back and forth, working off excess energy, fining himself down to performance level; a minor element of distortion crept into the margins of the image, and, cutting in the manual override, Murray fed his own corrections to Central until all was well.

Next came the main brain-wave amplification, delivering data in the emotional sphere: endocrine feeds, neural set, epithelial appercept, erogenous uptake. Diligently Murray keyed in each one. At first he received only a vague undifferentiated blur of formless background cerebration, but then, like intricate figures becoming clear in an elaborate oriental carpet, the specific characteristics of Nate's mental output began to clarify themselves: edginess, eagerness, horniness, alertness, intensity. A sense of Nate's formidable masculine strength came through. At this stage of the evening Murray still had a distinct awareness of himself as an entity independent of Nate, but that would change soon enough.

"Ready," Murray reported. "Holding awaiting Group cut-in."

He had to hold for fifteen intolerable minutes. He was always the quickest to synchronize. Then he had to sit and sweat, hanging on desperately to his balances and line-ups while he waited for the others. All around the circuit, the rest of them were still tinkering with their rigs, adjusting them with varying degrees of competence. He thought of Kay. At this moment making frantic adjustments, tuning herself to Serena as he had done to Nate.

"Group cut-in," Central said finally.

Murray closed the last circuits. Into his consciousness poured, in one wild rush, the mingled consciousnesses of Van, Dirk, Conrad, and Finn, hooked into him via Nate, and, less intensely because less directly, the consciousnesses of Kay, Maria, Lanelle, JoJo, and Nikki, funneled to him by way of their link to Serena. So all twelve of them were in synch. They had attained Group once again. Now the revels could begin.

Now. Nate approaching Serena. The magic moments of foreplay. That buzz of early excitement, that soaring erotic flight, taking everybody upward like a Beethoven adagio, like a solid hit of acid. Nate. Serena. San Diego. Their bedroom a glittering hall of mirrors. Refracted images everywhere. A thousand quivering breasts. Five hundred jutting cocks. Hands, eyes, tongues, thighs. The circular undulating bed, quivering, heaving. Murray, lying cocooned in his maze of sophisticated amplification equipment, receiving inputs at temples and throat and chest and loins, felt his palate growing dry, felt a pounding in his groin. He licked his lips. His hips began, of their own accord, a slow rhythmic thrusting motion. Nate's hands casually traversed the taut globes of Serena's bosom. Caught the rigid nipples between hairy fingers, tweaked them, thumbed them. Murray felt the firm nodules of engorged flesh with his own empty hands. The merger of identities was starting. He was becoming Nate, Nate was flowing into him, and he was all the others too, Van, JoJo, Dirk, Finn, Nikki, all of them, feedbacks oscillating in interpersonal whirlpools all along the line. Kay. He was part of Kay, she of him, both of them parts of Nate and Serena. Inextricably intertwined. What Nate experienced, Murray experienced. What Serena experienced, Kay experienced. When Nate's mouth descended to cover Serena's, Murray's tongue slid forward. And felt the moist tip of Serena's. Flesh against flesh, skin against skin. Serena was throbbing. Why not? Six men tonguing her at once. She was always quick to arouse, anyway. She was begging for it. Not that Nate was in any hurry: screwing was his thing, he always made a grand production out of it. As well he might, with ten close friends riding as passengers on his trip. Give is a show, Nate. Nate obliged. He was going down on her now. Inhaling. His stubbly cheeks against her satiny thighs. Oh, the busy tongue! Oh, the sighs and gasps! And then she engulfing him reciprocally. Murray hissed in delight. Her cunning little suctions, her jolly slithers and slides: a skilled fellatrice, that woman was. He trembled. He was fully into it now, sharing every impulse with Nate. *Becoming* Nate. Yes. Serena's beckoning body gaping for him. His waggling wand poised above her. The old magic of Group never diminishing. Nate doing all his tricks, pulling out the stops. When? Now. *Now.* The thrust. The quick sliding moment of entry. Ah! Ah! *Ah!* Serena simultaneously possessed by Nate, Murray, Van, Dirk, Conrad, Finn. Finn, Conrad, Dirk, Van, Murray, and Nate simultaneously possessing Serena. And, vicariously throbbing in rhythm with Serena, Kay, Maria, Lanelle, JoJo, Nikki. Kay. Kay. Kay. Through the sorcery of the crossover loop Nate was having Kay while he had Serena, Nate was having Kay, Maria, Lanelle, JoJo, Nikki all at once, they were being had by him, a soup of identities, an *olla podrida* of copulations, and as the twelve of them soared toward a shared and multiplied ecstasy Murray did something dumb. He thought of Kay.

He thought of Kay. Kay alone in her redwood bower, Kay with bucking hips and tossing hair and glistening droplets of sweat between her breasts, Kay hissing and shivering in Nate's simulated embrace. Murray tried to reach across to her through the Group loop, tried to find and isolate the discrete thread of self that was Kay, tried to chisel away the ten extraneous identities and transform this coupling into an encounter between himself and her. It was a plain violation of the spirit of Group; it was also impossible to achieve, since she had refused him permission to establish a special inner link between them that evening, and so at the moment she was accessible to him only as one facet of the enhanced and expanded Serena. At best he could grope toward Kay through Serena and touch the tip of her soul, but the contact was cloudy and uncertain. Instantly on to what he was trying to do, she petulantly pushed him away, at the same time submerging herself more fully in Serena's consciousness. Rejected, reeling, he slid off into confusion, sending jarring crosscurrents through the whole Group. Nate loosed a shower of irritation despite his heroic attempt to remain unperturbed, and pumped his way to climax well ahead of schedule, hauling everyone breathlessly along with him. As the orgasmic frenzy broke loose, Murray tried to re-enter the full linkage, but he found himself unhinged, disaffiliated, and mechanically emptied himself without any tremor of pleasure. Then it was over. He lay back, perspiring, feeling soiled, jangled, unsatisfied. After a few moments he uncoupled his equipment and went out for a cold shower.

Kay called half an hour later.

"You crazy bastard," she said. "What were you trying to do?"

He promised not to do it again. She forgave him. He brooded for two days, keeping out of Group. He missed sharing Conrad and JoJo, Klaus and Lois. The third day the Group chart marked him and Kay as that night's performers. He didn't want to let them all share her. It was stronger than ever, this nasty atavistic possessiveness. He didn't have to, of course. Nobody was forced to do Group. He could beg off and continue to sulk, and Dirk or Van or somebody would substitute for him tonight. But Kay wouldn't necessarily pass up her turn. She almost certainly wouldn't. He didn't like the options. If he made it with Kay as per group schedule, he'd be offering her to all the others. If he stepped aside, she'd do it with someone else. Might as well be the one to take her to bed, in that case. Faced with an ugly choice, he decided to stick to the original schedule.

He popped up to her place eight hours early. He found her sprawled on a carpet of redwood needles in a sun-dappled grove, playing with a stack of music cubes. Mozart tinkled in the fragrant air. "Let's go away somewhere tomorrow," he said. "You and me."

"You're still into you-and-me?"

"I'm sorry."

"Where do you want to go?"

He shrugged. "Hawaii. Afghanistan. Poland. Zambia. It doesn't matter. Just to be with you."

"What about Group?"

"They can spare us for a while."

She rolled over, lazily snaffled Mozart into silence, started a cube of Bach. "I'll go," she said. The Goldberg Variations transcribed for glockenspiel. "But only if we take our Group equipment along."

"It means that much to you?"

"Doesn't it to you?"

"I cherish Group," he said. "But it's not all there is to life. I can live without it for a while. I don't need it, Kay. What I need is you."

"That's obscene, Murray."

"No. It isn't obscene."

"It's boring, at any rate."

"I'm sorry you think so," he told her.

"Do you want to drop out of Group?"

I want us both to drop out of Group, he thought, and I want you to live with me. I can't bear to share you any longer, Kay. But he wasn't prepared to move to that level of confrontation. He said, "I want to stay in Group if it's possible, but I'm also interested in extending and developing some one-on-one with you."

"You've already made that excessively clear."

"I love you."

"You've said that before too."

"What do you want, Kay?"

She laughed, rolled over, drew her knees up until they touched her breasts, parted her thighs, opened herself to a stray shaft of sunlight. "I want to enjoy myself," she said.

He started setting up his equipment an hour before sunset. Because he was performing, the calibrations were more delicate than on an ordinary night. Not only did he have to broadcast a full range of control ratios to Central to aid the others in their tuning, he had to achieve a flawless balance of input and output with Kay. He went about his complex tasks morosely, not at all excited by the thought that he and Kay would shortly be making love. It cooled his ardor to know that Nate, Dirk, Van, Finn, Bruce, and Klaus would be having her too. Why did he begrudge it to them so? He didn't know. Such exclusivism, coming out of nowhere, shocked and disgusted him. Yet it wholly controlled him. Maybe I need help, he thought.

Group time now. Soft sweet ionized fumes drifting through the chamber of Eros. Kay was warm, receptive, passionate. Her eyes sparkled as she reached for him. They had made love five hundred times and she showed no sign of diminished interest. He knew he turned her on. He hoped he turned her on more than anyone else. He caressed her in all his clever ways, and she purred and wriggled and glowed. Her nipples stood tall: no faking that. Yet something was wrong. Not with her, with him. He was aloof, remote. He seemed to be watching the proceedings from a point somewhere outside himself, as though he were just a Group onlooker tonight, badly tuned in, not even as much a part of things as Klaus, Bruce, Finn, Van, Dirk. The awareness that he had an audience affected him for the first time. His technique, which depended more on finesse and grace than on fire and force, became a trap, locking him into a series of passionless arabesques and pirouettes. He was distracted, though he never had been before, by the minute telemetry tapes glued to the side of Kay's neck and the underside of her thigh. He found himself addressing silent messages to the other men. Here, Nate, how do you like that? Grab some haunch, Dirk. Up the old zaboo, Bruce. Uh. Uh. Ah. Oh.

Kay didn't seem to notice anything was amiss. She came three times in the first fifteen minutes. He doubted that he'd ever come at all. He plugged on, in and out, in and out, moving like a mindless piston. A sort of revenge on Group, he realized. You want to share Kay with me, okay, fellows, but this is all you're going to get. This. Oh. Oh. Oh. Now at last he felt the familiar climactic tickle, stepped down to a tenth of its normal intensity. He hardly noticed it when he came.

Kay said afterward, "What about that trip? Are we still going to go away somewhere tomorrow?"

"Let's forget it for the time being," he said.

He popped to Istanbul alone and spent a day in the covered bazaar buying cheap but intricate trinkets for every woman in Group. At nightfall he popped down to McMurdo Sound, where the merry Antarctic summer was at its height, and spent six hours on the polar ski slopes, coming away with wind-bronzed skin and aching muscles. In the lodge later he met an angular auburn-haired woman from Portugal and took her to bed. She was very good, in a heartless, mechanically proficient way. Doubtless she thought the same of him. She asked him whether he might be interested in joining her Group, which operated out of Lisbon and Ibiza. "I already have an affiliation," he said. He popped to Addis Ababa after breakfast, checked into the Hilton, slept for a day and a half, and went on to St. Croix for a night of reef-bobbing. When he popped back to California the next day he called Kay at once to learn the news.

"We've been discussing rearranging some of the Group couplings," she said. "Next week, what about you and Lanelle, me and Dirk?"

"Does that mean you're dropping me?"

"No, not at all, silly. But I do think we need some variety."

"Group was designed to provide us with all the variety we'd ever want."

"You know what I mean. Besides, you're developing an unhealthy fixation on me as isolated love-object."

"Why are you rejecting me?"

"I'm not. I'm trying to help you, Murray."

"I love you," he said.

"Love me in a healthier way, then."

That night it was the turn of Maria and Van. The next, Nikki and Finn. After them, Bruce and Mindy. He tuned in for all three, trying to erode his grief in nightly frenzies of lustful fulfillment. By the third night he was very tired and no less grief-smitten. He took the next night off. Then the schedule came up with the first Murray-Lanelle pairing.

He popped to Hawaii and set up his rig in her sprawling beachfront lanai on Molokai. He had bedded her before, of course. Everyone in Group had bedded everyone else during the preliminary months of compatibility testing. But then they all had settled into more or less regular pair-bonding, and he hadn't approached her since. In the past year the only Group woman he had slept with was Kay. By choice.

"I've always liked you," Lanelle said. She was tall, heavy-breasted, wide-shouldered, with warm brown eyes, yellow hair, skin the color of fine honey. "You're just a little crazy, but I don't mind that. And I love screwing Scorpios."

"I'm a Capricorn."

"Them too," she said. "I love screwing just about every sign. Except Virgos. I can't stand Virgos. Remember, we were supposed to have a Virgo in Group at the start. I blackballed him."

They swam and surfed for a couple of hours before doing the calibrating. The water was warm but a brisk breeze blew from the east, coming like a gust of bad news out of California. Lanelle nuzzled him playfully and then not so playfully in the water. She had always been an aggressive woman, a swaggerer, a strutter. Her appetites were enormous. Her eyes glistened with desire. "Come on," she said finally, tugging at him. They ran to the house and he began to adjust the equipment. It was still early. He thought of Kay and his soul drooped. What am I doing here, he wondered? He lined up the Group apparatus with nervous hands, making many errors. Lanelle stood behind him, rubbing her breasts against his bare back. He had to ask her to stop. Eventually everything was ready and she hauled him to the spongy floor with her, covering his body with hers. Lanelle always liked to be the one on top. Her tongue probed his mouth and her hands clutched his hips and she pressed herself against him, but although her body was warm and smooth and alive, he felt no onset of excitement, not a shred. She put her mouth to him but it was hopeless. He remained limp, dead, unable to function. With everyone tuned in and waiting. "What is it?" she whispered. "What should I do, love?" He closed his eyes and indulged in a fantasy of Kay coupling with Dirk, pure masochism, and it aroused him as far as a sort of half-erect condition, and he slithered into her like a prurient eel. She rocked her way to ecstasy above him. This is garbage, he thought. I'm falling apart. Kay. Kay. Kay.

Then Kay had her night with Dirk. At first Murray thought he would simply skip it. There was no reason, after all, why he had to subject himself to something like that if he expected it to give him pain. It had never been painful for him in the past when Kay did it with other men, inside Group or not, but since the onset of his jealousies everything was different. In theory the Group couples were interchangeable, one pair serving as proxies for all the rest each night, but theory and practice coincided less and less in Murray's mind these days. Nobody would be surprised or upset if he happened not to want to participate tonight. All during the day, though, he found himself obsessively fantasizing Kay and Dirk, every motion, every sound, the two of them facing each other, smiling, embracing, sinking down onto her bed, entwining, his hands sliding over her slender body, his mouth on her mouth, his chest crushing her small breasts, Dirk entering her, riding her, plunging, driving, coming, Kay coming, then Kay and Dirk arising, going for a cooling swim, returning to the bedroom, facing each other, smiling, beginning again. By late afternoon it had taken place so many times in his fevered imagination that he saw no risk in experiencing the reality of it; at least he could have Kay, if only at one remove, by doing Group tonight. And it might help him to shake off his obsessiveness. But it was worse than he imagined it could be. The sight of Dirk, all bulging muscles and tapering hips, terrified him; Dirk was ready for making love long before the foreplay started, and Murray somehow came to fear that he, not Kay, was going to be the target of that long rigid spear of his. Then Dirk began to caress Kay. With each insinuating touch of his hand it seemed some vital segment of Murray's relationship with Kay was being obliterated. He was forced to watch Kay through Dirk's eyes, her flushed face, her quivering nostrils, her moist, slack lips, and it killed him. As Dirk drove deep into her Murray coiled into a miserable fetal ball, one hand clutching his loins, the other clapped across his lips, thumb in his mouth. He couldn't stand it at all. To think that every one of them was having Kay at once. Not only Dirk. Nate, Van, Conrad, Finn, Bruce, Klaus, the whole male Group complement, all of them tuning in tonight for this novel Dirk-Kay pairing. Kay giving herself to all of them gladly, willingly, enthusiastically. He had to escape, now, instantly, even though to drop out of Group communion at this point would unbalance everyone's tuning and set up chaotic eddy-currents that might induce nausea or worse in the others. He didn't care. He had to save himself. He screamed and uncoupled his rig.

He waited two days and went to see her. She was at her exercises, floating like a cloud through a dazzling arrangement of metal rings and loops that dangled at constantly varying heights from the ceiling of her solarium. He stood below her, craning his neck. "It isn't any good," he said. "I want us both to withdraw from Group, Kay."

"That was predictable."

"It's killing me. I love you so much I can't bear to share you."

"So loving me means owning me?"

"Let's just drop out for a while. Let's explore the ramifications of one-on-one. A month, two months, six months, Kay. Just until I get this craziness out of my system. Then we can go back in."

"So you admit it's craziness."

"I never denied it." His neck was getting stiff. "Won't you please come down from those rings while we're talking?"

"I can hear you perfectly well from here, Murray."

"Will you drop out of Group and go away with me for a while?"

"No."

"Will you even consider it?"

"No."

"Do you realize that you're addicted to Group?" he asked.

"I don't think that's an accurate evaluation of the situation. But do *you* realize that you're dangerously fixated on me?"

"I realize it."

"What do you propose to do about it?"

"What I'm doing now," he said. "Coming to you, asking you to do a one-on-one with me."

"Stop it."

"One-on-one was good enough for the human race for thousands of years."

"It was a prison," she said. "It was a trap. We're out of the trap at last. You won't get me back in."

He wanted to pull her down from her rings and shake her. "I *love* you, Kay."

"You take a funny way of showing it. Trying to limit the range of my experience. Trying to hide me away in a vault somewhere. It won't work."

"Definitely no?"

"Definitely no."

She accelerated her pace, flinging herself recklessly from loop to loop. Her glistening nude form tantalized and infuriated him. He shrugged and turned away, shoulders slumping, head drooping. This was precisely how he had expected her to respond. No surprises. Very well. Very well. He crossed from the solarium into the bedroom and lifted her Group rig from its container. Slowly, methodically, he ripped it apart, bending the frame until it split, cracking the fragile leads, uprooting handfuls of connectors, crumpling the control panel. The instrument was already a ruin by the time Kay came in. "What are you *doing*?" she cried. He splintered the lovely gleaming calibration dials under his heel and kicked the wreckage of the rig toward her. It would take months before a replacement rig could be properly attuned and synchronized. "I had no choice," he told her sadly.

They would have to punish him. That was inevitable. But how? He waited at home, and before long they came to him, all of them, Nate, Van, Dirk, Conrad, Finn, Bruce, Klaus, Kay, Serena, Maria, JoJo, Lanelle, Nikki, Mindy, Lois, popping in from many quarters of the world, some of them dressed in evening clothes, some of them naked or nearly so, some of them unkempt and sleepy, all of them angry in a cold, tight way. He tried to stare them down. Dirk said, "You must be terribly sick, Murray. We feel sorry for you."

"We really want to help you," said Lanelle.

"We're here to give you therapy," Finn told him.

Murray laughed. "Therapy. I bet. What kind of therapy?"

"To rid you of your exclusivism," Dirk said. "To burn all the trash out of your mind."

"Shock treatment," Finn said.

"Keep away from me!"

"Hold him," Dirk said.

Quickly they surrounded him. Bruce clamped an arm across his chest like an iron bar. Conrad seized his hands and brought his wrists together behind his back. Finn and Dirk pressed up against his sides. He was helpless.

Kay began to remove her clothing. Naked, she lay down on Murray's bed, flexed her knees, opened her thighs. Klaus got on top of her.

"What the hell is this?" Murray asked.

Efficiently but without passion Kay aroused Klaus, and efficiently but without passion he penetrated her. Murray writhed impotently as their bodies moved together. Klaus made no attempt at bringing Kay off. He reached his climax in four or five minutes, grunting once, and rolled away from her, redfaced, sweating. Van took his place between Kay's legs.

"No," Murray said. "Please, no."

Inexorably Van had his turn, quick, impersonal. Nate was next. Murray tried not to watch, but his eyes would not remain closed. A strange smile glittered on Kay's lips as she gave herself to Nate. Nate rose. Finn approached the bed.

"No!" Murray cried and lashed out in a backwards kick that sent Conrad screaming across the room. Murray's hands were free. He twisted and wrenched himself away from Bruce. Dirk and Nate intercepted him as he rushed toward Kay. They seized him and flung him to the floor.

"The therapy isn't working," Nate said.

"Let's skip the rest," said Dirk. "It's no use trying to heal him. He's beyond hope. Let him stand up."

Murray got cautiously to his feet. Dirk said, "By unanimous vote, Murray, we expel you from Group for unGrouplike attitudes and especially for your unGrouplike destruction of Kay's rig. All your Group privileges are canceled." At a signal from Dirk, Nate removed Murray's rig from its container and reduced it to unsalvageable rubble. Dirk said, "Speaking as your friend, Murray, I suggest you think seriously about undergoing a total personality reconstruct. You're in trouble, do you know that? You need a lot of help. You're a mess."

"Is there anything else you want to tell me?" Murray asked.

"Nothing else. Goodbye, Murray."

They started to go out. Dirk, Finn, Nate, Bruce, Conrad, Klaus, Van. JoJo. Nikki, Serena, Maria, Lanelle, Mindy. Lois. Kay was the last to leave. She stood by the door, clutching her clothes in a small crumpled bundle. She seemed entirely unafraid of him. There was a peculiar look of—was it tenderness? pity?—on her face. Softly she said, "I'm sorry it had to come to this, Murray. I feel so unhappy for you. I know that what you did wasn't a hostile act. You did it out of love. You were all wrong, but you were doing it out of love." She walked toward him and kissed him lightly, on the cheek, on the tip of the nose, on the lips. He didn't move. She smiled. She touched his arm. "I'm so sorry," she murmured. "Goodbye, Murray." As she went through the door she looked back and said, "Such a damned shame. I could have loved you, you know? I could really have loved you."

He had told himself that he would wait until they all were gone before he let the tears flow. But when the door had closed behind Kay, he discovered his eyes remained dry. He had no tears. He was altogether calm. Numb. Burned out.

After a long while he put on fresh clothing and went out. He popped to London, found that it was raining there, and popped to Prague, where there was something stifling about the atmosphere, and went on to Seoul, where he had barbecued beef and kimchi for dinner. Then he popped to New York. In front of a gallery on Lexington Avenue he picked up a complaisant young girl with long black hair. "Let's go to a hotel," he suggested, and she smiled and nodded. He registered for a six-hour stay. Upstairs, she undressed without waiting for him to ask. Her body was smooth and supple, flat belly, pale skin, high full breasts. They lay down together and, in silence, without preliminaries, he took her. She was eager and responsive. Kay, he thought. Kay. Kay. You are Kay. A spasm of culmination shook him with unexpected force.

"Do you mind if I smoke?" she said a few minutes later.

"I love you," he said.

"What?"

"I love you."

"You're sweet."

"Come live with me. Please. Please. I'm serious."

"What?"

"Live with me. Marry me."

"*What?*"

"There's only one thing I ask. No Group stuff. That's all. Otherwise you can do as you please. I'm wealthy. I'll make you happy. I love you."

"You don't even know my name."

"I love you."

"Mister, you must be out of your head."

"Please. Please."

"A lunatic. Unless you're trying to make fun of me."

"I'm perfectly serious, I assure you. Live with me. Be my wife."

"A lunatic," she said. "I'm getting out of here!" She leaped up and looked for her clothes. "Jesus, a madman!"

"No," he said, but she was on her way, not even pausing to get dressed, running helter-skelter from the room, her pink buttocks flashing like beacons as she made her escape. The door slammed. He shook his head. He sat rigid for half an hour, an hour, some long timeless span, thinking of Kay, thinking of Group, wondering what they'd be doing tonight, whose turn it was. At length he rose and put on his clothes and left the hotel. A terrible restlessness assailed him. He popped to Karachi and stayed ten minutes. He popped to Vienna. To Hangchow. He didn't stay. Looking for what? He didn't know. Looking for Kay? Kay didn't exist. Looking. Just looking. Pop. Pop. Pop.

THOMAS N. SCORTIA

Flowering Narcissus

Honcho is dreaming. It is a simple, brutal dream. He stands spread-eagled, feeling the potency in his muscles and the cold touch of leather against his bare loins. He's proud of the muscularity of his thighs and buttocks. Every time he stands in a bar (as he does now in his dream), he flexes the muscles, feeling the heavy indentation in his glutei maximi. The chicks watch him out of the corner of their eyes, their gaze telling him that they think he's a real stud. Now one gets up and comes toward him, wide hips swaying, breasts thrusting. He grabs her by the hair at the nape of the neck and pulls her head back brutally. He smiles at her, exposing stained yellow teeth. Below the half-sleeves of his jacket his massive biceps bulge, the veins writhing like ropes. He is going to push her to the floor and use his boot on those inflated boobs, but . . .

It all dissolves.

He is lying with his eyes closed. He feels the pressure of

sheets against the hair on his torso. He tries to open his eyes, but they seem glued together. He is cold, colder than he has ever been in his life in spite of the warmth the sheets are exuding. He doesn't remember being this cold, certainly not in California, certainly not in the dead of summer with the heat devils dancing over the blacktop of the freeways and his wheels kicking up a cloud of dust and grit behind him.

Then he remembers. That kooky egghead in Berkeley. He needed the bread and the ad in the *Barb* sounded nutty enough so that he thought he could con the gink out of a few bills. Only the little guy had been legit; he even taught at U. C. and he wanted Honcho to go through with it. It was perfectly safe, he said. Three bills for just going to sleep for a week. Well, Honcho decided, trying to unglue his eyes, the week was over and he'd have enough money for a couple of lids and a brace of poppers for the club run the end of the month.

"Damn it," he yells when he tries to move and finds his arms strapped to his sides. "What kind of trip is this?"

From some distance he hears the sound of feet scraping against the floor, then the squeak of a door. Now somebody is in the room and he senses a presence crossing, bending over him. Something moist swabs at his eyes. They burn like fire but suddenly the lids are no longer glued and he can part them.

Honcho opens his eyes slowly, painfully because the light hurts. It feels as though he has been holding his lids tightly compressed for hours. The air fills with spots of light and crawling shadows. Beyond these he makes out a shape. Human? He can't tell, but he knows it is probably the face of the little egghead who has put him in this trip. He waits for the image to clear and, sure enough, he begins to make out the shape. It's a man's head, he sees. Bald, not a trace of hair. Beyond this he cannot yet make out facial details.

He closes his eyes and tries to rub them. His hands are still bound. The man above him makes a movement and his hands are free. He scrubs vigorously at his eyes, ignoring the copious flow of tears. Then he opens his eyes. He can see again. Purple and black spots still float before his eyes, but he can see. The face above him swims into focus. It is not the face he expects.

"Who the hell are you?" he demands.

"Take it easy," the man says. "You'll be all right."

Honcho realizes that he has assumed it is a man, but the voice is high and gentle-sounding, not at all masculine. The head is bald, shaved maybe, and the build is slight. He (she) is not over five three and slim to the point of emaciation. The body is covered by a single loose-fitting tunic. There are no signs of sex in the clothing cut, no indication of breasts. Honcho decides that it must be a man, even though he can see no trace of beard.

Honcho sits up and flexes his biceps. He laughs, feeling the sudden animal pleasure of being alive. The bald gink looks at him with wide eyes. Man, he thinks, ain't you ever seen a guy with a man's build. Then he digs. The gink is looking at him with admiration and Honcho says to himself, That kind of scene? Ugh. Eat your heart out, baby. And he feels damned good.

"Where's the professor?" Honcho demands.

"Professor?" the little man says. "Oh, you mean Dr. Liebowicz?"

"That's right. The little ginch with the four eyes."

"He's dead," the man says. "He's been dead a long time."

"Hey, baby, don't give me that shit," Honcho says, springing from the bed and grabbing the little guy by the loose cloth of his tunic. "Nobody cons me, sweetie."

The little man pushes Honcho's hand away, not so much with strength as with the sudden solemn authority of his large eyes. "It's true," he says. "Liebowicz is dead. He died in prison over a century ago."

"Oh, God," Honcho says and sinks down to the bed. A century ago. "Somebody's going to pay for this," he yells.

"Somebody's going to fork over lots of bread. It was only supposed to be a week."

"One hundred fifteen years and . . . ah . . . four months," the little guy says.

"Who the hell are you?"

"CTX-25, series ten," the little guy says.

"What kind of a name is that for a human?" Honcho demands.

"I am not human," the little guy named CTX-25 says.

"You sure ain't no Martian."

"No," CTX-25 says. "I was built."

"Huh, call that a build," Honcho says.

"By humans," the little guy says, dropping his eyes and making a funny motion of respect with his right hand, two fingers extended. "Before the plague," he says.

"Hey," Honcho says. "You're coming on too fast. What plague?"

"Why, the plague that destroyed the human race," CTX-25 says and before Honcho can answer he leaves the way he came.

Honcho feels weak and he falls back onto the bed. He is suddenly scared. He doesn't like it one bit. Somebody is having a great day with him, he decides. He yawns and says, "What a hell of a note; sleepy after sleeping a century." But he falls back, his head touches a pillow, and he is sound asleep, filling the air with rasping snores. He does not dream now.

When he wakes up, he yells out, "Damn it, what do you have to do to get some chow around here?"

The door magically opens and another little guy wheels in a cart with a steaming steak, a big baked potato awash with sour cream, peas and a frothy mug of beer. "You read my mind," Honcho says to the little guy who is not CTX-25.

"That's right," the little guy says. Then, "I brought you a viewer." He points to a thing that looks like a portable TV on the cart and then, without saying another word, leaves.

Honcho dives in. He is not one for niceties. He rapes the steak, mauls the potato, gulps the beer, and smears the grease away from his lips with the hairy back of his hand. Then he starts to fiddle with the viewer.

There are two knobs. One turns on the gadget; the other presses inward to flip view after view on the screen. There are old newspaper clippings about Liebowicz, who is accused of illegal experimentation on humans. He is tried and convicted while a bunch of deadhead students demonstrate outside the courtroom. The court psychiatrist decides he is spaced out and they send him to Vacaville, where eventually he is killed when one of the other inmates doesn't like the way he parts his skin. There's some crap about building a place to keep the sleeping Honcho. They even have Honcho's biography and a picture of him, mounted on his competition Dunstall-Norton 750, leering out at the camera. (What a pile that machine cost him, a beautiful hog and probably all rust now.) He can't believe the biography. He wonders who fed the newspapers all that Sunday-school crap. Boy-wonder mechanic, cyclist, man among men. (Well, sure, but not that goody-good.) He flips the knob in disgust.

There's stuff about new developments in biochemistry. Some doubledome named Whitfield creates artificial tissue in the lab, and later a guy called Nobel Laureate Valdez builds something called an android. There are pictures, and Honcho recognizes something that looks like CTX-25. (The article says they're sexless, which to Honcho makes no sense, and his original suspicions about CTX-25 return. Imagine a world peopled by artificial faggots. He laughs out loud at that thought.)

After that he reads about the war between the Chinks and the Russkies and how one side or the other starts to use virus warfare. Only it gets out of hand and sweeps the world. There's one final item. By now apparently the androids are publishing the newspapers, because the final item says, "Last human being dies." After that there is nothing. The dateline is seventy-five years after Honcho began his big sleep.

When CTX-25 comes in later, Honcho is in a brown mood. "That's a lot of crap," he says, pointing at the viewer. "Ain't it?" he asks hopefully.

"No, it is history," CTX-25 says.

"You mean I'm the only human alive in the world?" he demands.

CTX-25 asks, "Are you feeling better? Is the food all right?"

"Damn it, I asked you a question," Honcho roars.

"We'll answer your questions later," CTX-25 says with a pale smile. "We have to make sure you're in good health."

"I can chew up a pansy like you and spit out the pieces," Honcho says.

CTX-25 hands him some clothes. Honcho is delighted. Jackboots with a chain across the insteps, just like he used to have. Black leather chaps and Levi's, a shirt and black leather vest topped off by a leather cap filled with badges. The slogans on the badges don't make much sense, but the image is good. The Levi's are neat and clean and pressed. While CTX-25 watches, Honcho rumples them and drags them across the floor. He thinks maybe he should christen them like they do for the new guys in the Satan's Wheels but it takes too damned long for them to dry. So he puts them on that way. A few days and they'll feel decent, he decides.

CTX-25 takes him down to a gym where a couple other of the sexless ginches are waiting. They put him through all sorts of tests on what they call a dynamometer. They make him run on a treadmill, listen to his heart, wire him up to a fancy gadget that flashes out patterns on an oscilloscope. While they watch and chatter among themselves, he grabs an overhead bar and chins himself thirty-five times. Not as good as usual, but the little guys are impressed.

"Look," he says, "I played your game, but you guys owe me something. From what you tell me, you were built to serve humans."

"That's right," CTX-25 says.

"That still operates, don't it?"

"That's right," the android says.

"Okay," Honcho says. "Then I ain't happy the way things are going. You guys gotta get me what I want."

"Food?" one of them asks.

"Hell, no," Honcho says. "I want a pad. I'll tell you what I want. Then I want a hog."

"Hog," CTX-25 says. "An animal?"

"A bike, damn it," Honcho says, "and make sure there's someplace to ride it. You got roads, ain't you?"

"There will be roads," they promise him.

"And a babe," Honcho says. "A twist, a snatch."

"A woman," CTX-25 says with a vague smile. "We are working on that."

"See that you get it right." Honcho pauses. "And none of your androids. I don't go for that."

"There is another in sleep," CTX-25 says. "We are reviving her. I think you will like her."

"Huh," Honcho says. "I damn well better."

The next day CTX-25 takes him down an elevator and out in front of the building. There, leaning on its kick-stand, is a bike. "You read my mind," he yells excitedly, running over to the machine.

"Precisely," CTX-25 says, but Honcho ignores him. It's the very same, the Dunstall-Norton 750, just the way he remembers it. His hand caresses the reshaped exhaust ports with their gleaming metal. He can see where the combustion chambers have been resphered when he looks into the engine. He knows that they're five millimeters greater in diameter and he knows all the other things that have been done to the standard Norton: the steeper inlet valve angles, the larger inlet valves and ports, the greater compression ratio. Then he sees the nick on the throttle handle and the pit on the accelerator dial and he knows this isn't just another machine.

"How the hell?" he yells. "It's my own baby."

"We tried to duplicate it completely," CTX-25 says proudly. "We're very good at that."

Honcho mounts the cracked leather seat, opens the pet-cock, and throws his weight on the starter. The engine turns over with a roar and he grips the throttle with his left hand and starts to feed it gas. The smell fills his nose like whiskey and he feels his heart race with the excitement. Ignoring CTX-25, he kicks up the stand, engages the clutch, and he's off, roaring down the concrete incline and out onto a broad concrete road that circles away from the low building and into the trees.

The wind is whipping past his head and biting into his eyes. He wishes he had goggles, but he feeds the hog gas and watches the needle climb. The hydraulic front shocks are singing and the whole beast feels like something alive between his legs. It feels like an extension of his meat, and he hugs the frame with his knees, remembering the excitement the last time the Wheels went to Monterey on a run and they strung the gremmy up by his thumbs to one of the trees and worked him over while Seven-times Cindy came over and emptied her beer all over his bare butt. Far out.

Only the road doesn't go anywhere. He circles, and suddenly there is the sprawling white building and there's CTX-25 waiting for him, a cold smile on his face. "You can take the back road next time," he says. "That goes into the city." Honcho sees that a ribbon of concrete runs to the rear and arrows out toward a distant hill. There's no sign of a city and he assumes that it is over the hill.

"I'll just do that now," he says.

"No," CTX-25 says. "I have another surprise for you."

Honcho reluctantly dismounts and kicks down the stand on the bike. The machine smells excitingly of hot metal and gasoline. He follows CTX-25 up the steps into the building. They walk down the long corridor and downstairs into another level. CTX-25 gestures at a door and Honcho pushes through into a room very much like the one he first awoke in. There's a bed, and several pieces of cryptic apparatus stand in the corner. In the bed is a form.

She's still unconscious, her huge breasts rising and falling under the sheet. The nipples make sharp indentations in the fabric. She's big, Honcho sees, maybe as tall as he is, with wide amazon hips and a big face with sensuous lips and long black hair. She looks like quite a piece and he turns to CTX-25.

"Is this another of your kind?" he demands.

"No, she's not android," CTX-25 says. "She will awaken soon and then she's yours."

Honcho licks his lips and feels his groin tense. Suddenly he's horny as hell and he can't wait. She looks like every doll he's ever had. He knows every contour of her body and the way she'll kiss and ball and he can't wait.

CTX-25 prods him out of the room and conducts him back to his quarters. They're new quarters now with deep leather chairs and bike pictures on the wall and a refrigerator with beer and Dago red. There's a chest with smokes and poppers and a lid of grass. Somebody has scrawled "Acapulco Gold" across the label and he opens it and sniffs it. The real stuff, he decides, and not cut with a lot of syrup.

"When's that piece gonna wake up?" he demands.

"Soon," CTX-25 assures him and leaves him to himself.

There's a hi-fi at one end of the room and he finds a Led Butterfly album he likes. (Where did they get the thing? he wonders.) With the music blasting around him, he pours himself a glass of Dago red. Everybody tells him the stuff should be drunk hot but he likes it cold and bitter. He kicks off his boots, wiggles his toes in their sweat-stained socks to the music, and starts to get high. After a while he rolls himself a joint and alternates between puffs and a gulp of the wine. In no time he is floating, not tripping out exactly . . . but floating.

He thinks about the snatch below who must now be awake and wonders how the hell she got in the middle of the next century. He feels a kind of gratitude to CTX-25 and he smiles to himself contemptuously. Poor bastard, never humping it.

What a way to live, but he apparently understands what Honcho needs. He begins to feel the secondary effects of the pot and a kind of suspicion begins to grow.

Just what's in it for the creep? he wonders. He's given Honcho everything he wants and now he's found Honcho a woman. Of course, his kind was built to serve humans. Only there ain't any more humans, none except Honcho and the piece below. Which brings him around to the question again. Why?

And suddenly Honcho knows. He spits wine halfway across the room and yells, "That bastard." Of course he'll get Honcho a broad. Why? Because there are no humans to serve and he and his kind are built to serve humans. They need it like a head needs his fix. So, where does that leave Honcho? Honcho and the broad? Of course! The bastard expects Honcho to father a whole horde of sniveling snotnose kids just so CTX-25 and his crowd will have somebody to serve.

"Not damned likely," Honcho announces to the walls, drowning out even Led Butterfly. "That ain't my scene, baby," he tells nobody in particular. He's mad now and if CTX-25 were in the room he would deck the ball-less wonder. He throws the half-filled glass at one of the hi-fi speakers and starts to pull on his boots.

He stands up and finds he's weaving on his feet. No matter. He knows what to do. He'll cut the ground right from under them and wind it all up with an orgy of laying that'll leave them panting. He puts on his cap and stumbles out into the hall. There's no one around, which is just fine. He walks the length of the hall, finds the steps, and goes down and down to the level where the broad is. He finds the room and pushes open the door.

She's asleep, her heavy breasts rising and falling regularly. Part of the sheet has twisted around her, outlining her full figure, and Honcho licks his lips at what he sees. One heavy thigh protrudes from the cover and he marvels at the heavy musculature. He can imagine those heavy thighs tightening around his waist as he drives in and possesses her violently.

She opens her eyes and says, "Hey, man, what makes?"

"You know what those bastards are up to?" he says dreamily.

"You're high," she accuses.

"So what?" Honcho says. "That doesn't keep me from knowing they want us to start breeding a lot of brats so they can have a human race to worship and serve."

"Baby, you can get yourself another girl," she says. "I'm not about to be anybody's bitch."

"I got other plans for you," Honcho says. "We gotta get out of here."

"I'm for that," she says.

"What's your name?" he says.

"Mary," she says. "Ain't that a laugh?"

"Get your clothes on," he says. "I got a beast outside and we'll split before they know we're gone."

"Ain't got no clothes," she says. "What the hell, who needs clothes?" She gets to her feet and wraps the sheet around her.

They make it out of the door and down the corridor, up one flight of stairs, and out into the cold night where the hog waits patiently, leaning against its stand.

"Man," she says, "that's a beast. What'd it set you back?"

"Originally?" he says. "Hell, I saved for three years. You don't get that kind of bike cheap."

He mounts the seat and she wriggles on behind him. The sheet is wrapped tightly around her lush figure but he can feel her heat against his body, even through the leather vest. She has a kind of raunchy female smell about her that excites him. He reaches around and gropes in a strategic spot. She moans as his hand closes brutally on her. She's all woman, Honcho assure himself, and she's just what he needs to take the edge off his appetite.

He throws his weight on the starter and the Norton comes alive. She grabs onto him as he throws in the clutch and they speed down the concrete ramp and take the road that circles around the building. As they leave the area, they arrow through a grove of trees and the road stretches like a ribbon before them, the moonlight painting it a scabrous yellow.

He guns the machine and watches the speedometer creep upward: sixty, seventy, eighty. There is no sign of pursuit, and he roars his defiance into the wind that is biting his face. Behind him she clutches his chest and shivers. She starts to insinuate her fingers past the vest and into his shirt, rubbing the hair on his chest until he is roaring no longer with defiance but with sheer lust.

Damn, he feels like Gene Romero tooling the Sacramento track. All balls and a mile wide. They're halfway to the rise now. On the other side, if he can believe the little creep CTX-25, is the city and he wonders what he will do there. Her hands are all over him now. She's excited and the excitement is spreading to him. He sees a grove of trees ahead and he says, What the hell, to himself. He slows, kicks at the ground with his left foot, which is partly protected by a metal mask over the boot, and tears into the grove. His hand bears down on the brake and they almost fly over the bars as he stops, dismounts, kills the engine, and kicks the stand.

"What's up, stud?" she challenges. Her grin tells him she knows what is up.

He grabs her, yanks her from the seat, and *pulls* her to the ground. The sheet falls half away and his hands are brutally over her. He seizes her head, forcing it down while he jerks at the lacing on his chaps. Man, he thinks, this is what I've been waiting for.

Only there's a beam of light plunging out of the sky and outlining them. It's some kind of whirlybird, he thinks, and they're after them. "Honcho," a voice says from on high. "Come back. You don't have to do this."

He bundles her back in the sheet, ignores the loose lacing on his leather chaps, and they're back on the machine. The thing roars and they're on the road while the machine overhead flops clumsily, following them while the light shoots down and the voice pleads with him to return.

They're approaching the crest of the hill and he knows that

if he can get over it they can dodge the flopter and hide. At the crest of the hill he sees that they won't make it. It's all a camouflage, a fake. There's nothing beyond the hill, no road, no city, no nothing.

The bike leaps out into space. He can see a place to bring it down, if he's lucky, a flat spot, graveled and level. Like ole Knievel, he thinks. Hell, jump twenty automobiles. This takes guts.

Then they hit and the tires spit gravel. The machine flips into the air and he is turning slowly, agonizingly. He hits and all is pain and darkness.

Honcho is dreaming. It is the same dream, a brutal dream of gross masculine sexuality. His eyes are gummed together but shortly someone swabs them and he opens his eyes to the same room. CTX-25 is waiting for him.

"You bastard," he says. "You caught us. If you think I'm going to be a breeding stud for you—"

"No, we didn't catch you," CTX-25 says.

"What the hell," Honcho says, ignoring him. "Am I hurt?"

"No, the body is perfectly sound. That body at least."

"What's that gibberish supposed to mean."

"You were killed," CTX-25 says sadly.

"Bullshit," Honcho says. "I'm more alive than you are."

"This Honcho is," CTX-25 says.

"You're out of your mind," Honcho says.

"No," CTX-25 says. "We were forced to clone you again."

"Clone? What does clone mean?"

CTX-25 tells him. The Honcho that Liebowicz threw into suspended animation did not live. That is, he could not revive. There were no other humans available to them. There was only one solution. Take a single cell, this time from the esophagus. It contains all of the chromosomes necessary to produce the complete individual. They grew a new Honcho. But wanting him to be completely human, they scanned the sleeping mind, impressed the new brain by their techniques with the old personality. For practical purposes, the new Honcho was a continuation of the old—all the good, all the bad.

"When Honcho died in the cycle crash, we had to do it all over again."

"What about the babe?" he demands. She survived, he is told. Is she deformed, crippled? he wants to know. No, their science is equal to such injuries.

"Damn it, I want her," he says.

"Don't you understand who she is?" CTX-25 wants to know.

"She's another one who survived or maybe you re-created her. Never mind, she's all broad."

"Only one living creature survived." CTX-25 insists.

"I survived," Honcho roars, "and so did she."

"No," CTX says slowly, watching his face. "She came from the same process you did."

Honcho stares at him. A sickness arises in him. He cannot accept what the android is telling him.

"It's easy," CTX-25 is saying. "At one stage in the development, the fetus has the potentiality of either sex."

"That's queer!"

"Do you want to be alone?" CTX-25 says, and he leaves Honcho to contemplate the problems of this, his third life. He thinks for a long while, and while he thinks he remembers the full, exciting body. Fake or not, it was a damned good one. His hand massages himself and he thinks, Well, what the hell, better than mother thumb and her four daughters.

He is quite prepared when the door opens and she enters the room. He had thought she looked familiar and now he knows. Hell, how can he be disgusted with himself? The idea sort of appeals in a way. He always had a good opinion of himself.

"You all right?" she asks.

"Come here," he says.

She walks over to the bed and sits down, looking at him

with eyes that say animal things. He rises until he is sitting upright and grabs at her.

"I thought you'd never do that," she says.

He kisses her, bruising her lips with his intensity while his hand slides down and finds the secret place he knows. She is all woman, that's for sure.

"Man," he says fiercely. Then he corrects himself and says, "Babe, we're really going to make it with each other."

"We sure as hell are," she says, returning the fierce urgency of his kiss.

"We are really gonna make it, you and me," he says again. "Baby, we were made for each other."

"You can say that again," she says, pulling away from his lips and lowering her head to bite painfully at his distended nipples.

JON STOPA

Kiddy-Lib

Sure, I ain't got a job. Who the hell wants to hire a teddy bear?

I mean, after all, I was *the* Teddi Bear. The damned kids turned their backs on me after the revolution. That's what hurt most. Said I was too childish. The schmucks!

Say, did you see me in my Teddi Bear suit? I still got it.

Here. They let me keep it, but it upsets 'em. Just hold the top parts while I—Omph, these must be shrinking. There, now give me the jacket. Now the head mask. Careful, don't let the stick-strips touch.

Heh, heh, how's that? See, being a chubby little shrimp isn't all bad. Show biz is crummy. But there's always a place for guys like me. I keep forgetting, there used to be.

Oh, well, meet Teddi Bear! Captain of the good ship *Magic Dragon!* Known and loved by millions! Honored and respected. But it's gone now. A sad, sad shame.

Ah, but I sang! I danced! I can still do it; watch this. A

backover flip—oof! Oh, that hurt. This suit *is* damned tight. Yeah, so okay, so maybe I am a wee bit out of condition.

You know, right down at the heart, the reason this hurt so is that I really do love kids. Yeah, I know I snatched a big bundle while I was Teddi Bear. But do you think I could stand the mindless scripts I used, day in, day out, year after year, if I didn't love the little buggers?

Look, you schmuck! You came to learn a little history. So keep a civil tongue in your head. Remember, DOMpa is perfectly legit.

At least now. Big deal. Anyway, that's how my historic bit got started. In those days DOMpa was underground, the only part of the grand coalition that never managed to surface after the sexual revolution. We were really bitter too.

You know, someday they're going to let me out of here. You wait. Anyway, we couldn't understand why we were the only ones still being picked on. We done our bit turning on the straights. Women's lib, gay lib, the rest. Why kick us cause we dug kids?

Judge Pollyester socked it to us at every turn. First time I met him I really was in a pickle.

We had just been busted. None too gently, either. The blimp shuddered and swayed to a stop. The fat cop unlocked Ginny-O's cell. "Come on, sweetie," he said, "you're a nice little girl. Let me take your hand."

"Don't touch me, you dirty bourgeois hippie pig!" she snarled, pulling away. Lotta grit for an eleven-year-old! The proverbial lump of pride came to my throat. Trouble is, it contained my gorge. I could hear the angry mob outside howling. They were parents.

Screaming, Ginny-O fought back, pulling hair and biting fingers. "Damn you!" hollered the cop. Two more came over, and the three carried the little wildcat out.

I, being older, and having more sense—mainly of self-preservation went quietly. The crowd's raw fury hit me as I climbed down. I shuddered. "Come on, lover boy," said one of the gay cops, "get on the streetraft." He shoved, roughly.

The raft slid across the fenced-in compound to an ancient stone federal building. Boy, was I glad there was a fence there.

Inside, we were separated. I ended up in a cell overlooking the angry mob, feeling sorry for myself and very scared. Me, Teddi Bear! Caught in the act. I was done!

The tumult out there grew louder. Imperceptibly it changed. I was moping on my cot, when I heard the cry: *"Free Teddi Bear! Free Teddi Bear!"*

I jumped to the window. A vast throng of unruly kids had joined the crowd at the fence. The outnumbered adults were milling about, uncertain. They had been drowned out by the shrill new chant.

The mob of kids swiftly swelled, until it was ten to one. My fans. They weren't forgetting me! At some unseen signal the kids suddenly leaped at the adults, like a school of maddened piranhas. Isolated parents went down under the weight of the small bodies. They didn't get up. In spite of myself, I shuddered. The surviving adults joined together, beating a hasty retreat.

"Free Teddi Bear!"

The cell door clanged open. Before I could protest, two fuzz dragged me out and down to the judge's chamber. "You better bow and cringe a lot," said one. "Judge Pollyester can't stand smartasses."

"Where's my lawy—" He shoved me in before I could finish. The room's somber mood cowed me. I was grabbed by cops on each side and marched past empty wooden benches. Gothic windows along the front wall let in filtered gray light. Witches had been condemned to death in places like this.

Our parade came to a halt below Judge Pollyester's desk. I took the blue meanie's advice. I cowered a lot. The judge glared sourly at me. There were large yellow flowers woven into his thin gray hair, which hung down past the shoulders of his black robe. With one clawlike hand he fiddled with his worn love beads.

"Don't you ever take off that teddy bear outfit?" he cackled.

"I don't have anything else to wear," I said reasonably.

"Then why don't you take off your mask?"

"Er— I don't want to lose it."

"Well, take it off in my court!" he shouted.

"Aw, gee." But it was no use. I took it off.

"Now then," he said, closing his robe tightly against the chill of the room. "We got you dead to rights, you dirty old man. Want to tell us exactly what you were doing on the top of that hill?" His broken old voice was like a rusty ax.

"Dancing," I said.

"Dancing?" The judge spluttered.

"Well, yes." My courage was rising. The kids' chants were beginning to penetrate here. "We were rehearsing a number for my show. Miss—" I stopped, panicking. I had never asked Ginny-O her last name. Hastily I said, "Say, what is going on? Where's my goddam lawyer?"

The judge glared down balefully. "This isn't a trial. We're not arresting you, you scum. Just answer the questions. I've got a special interest in wiping out buggers like you."

"We're not buggers! That's legal."

"Never mind." He leaned back, pulling his hands back into his sleeves. "Now then, we know you were at the DOMpa orgy in the Essex House when we busted the joint. Talk your way out of that."

"Come on, give." One of the cops poked me in the ribs. Thank God for those kids out there! These guys really hated me.

"Gee, you mean to say there was an orgy there? I didn't know that! Me, I was there holding an audition for Ginny-O. Terrible, really. A bunch of hoodlums invaded it. No police there to protect us too. Never around when you need them, are they?"

The judge rose abruptly, his face gaunt. "Get out," he said, his voice tight. He pointed a bony finger at the door. "*Get out!* I know who you are now. Sooner or later we'll get you."

Shrugging, I said, "Where's the girl?"

"The girl?"

"Yes. Ginny-O." That was brazen. With those kids out there howling, I could afford to be. The pigs were letting me go because they were scared.

"You're not being fair," whined the judge. He slumped back. "Okay. She can go too."

I laughed. Putting my mask back on, I turned my back on Judge Pollyester and strode out. The blue meanies had the girl waiting for me at the door. Together we went out to greet the cheering mob.

The revolution really had started the day before. Up till then DOMpa had been an ineffectual organization. Hell, it couldn't protect a wolf from grandma. We just got together and sang and smoked a bit. But it was at that meeting that I got the idea that started it all.

It was a brisk spring day. I entered the venerable old chrome and glass Essex House. You remember the place. I handed my coat to Bidwell, the butler.

"Your hat—I mean your mask, sir?" He coughed politely.

"Er, no, thank you. I'll wear it. I have to go to rehearsals later."

"Very good, sir," he said vaguely. "You'll find the others in the Peachy-Keen Room."

Great butler, Bidwell. Too bad they don't make them like that any more. I stepped into the ancient manually operated elevator and pushed the button. The door closed, and I barely yanked my plastic broadsword back in time. A damned bunch of medieval freaks had caught the eye of the fashion industry. You know, armor, chain mail, codpieces, and junk like that. That sword was the only stuff I wore.

Upstairs, the place looked like a medieval revel. People were clicking and bouncing off each other as they moved in their plastic casings. I joined Freddy Operr—a DOMpa old-timer, a really dear man. He was telling the group about the Kaelson Process, which his lab had just perfected.

Everyone is familiar with it now, but at the time it was brand new. I can remember him pacing back and forth, a long black saber flapping against his leg. He was wearing black leatherette.

"Do you realize what this means?" He stabbed the air with two fingers.

"Oh, man, too much," said Levan, an old smartass. Never got along with him. " 'Splain, baby. Tell us what it means."

"Arg," said Freddy. He was a shy guy, easily put down. "Well, the process can take any growing process and speed it up or stop it entirely. Hell, it'll even reverse it. Up till now the various maturation processes affected the whole body. With the Kaelson Process we key the various hormones and genetic material on a molecular level with chemical tags. They affect only the parts we want to change. Say you didn't want a beard. We'd regress it back to peach fuzz, but the rest of you wouldn't be affected."

"No beards, huh," said Levan, sarcastically. "Gosh, wow!"

"Shut up, you schmuck!" I leaped at the gray old goat's bod with my fist cocked. Unfortunately, my broadsword took this moment to place itself between my legs. I flopped on my face.

"Heh, heh," I said, looking up at the boot Levan held above my head. "Wanna shine, mister?"

"Shine? Hell, I've been waiting for years to kick in your ugly puss!"

"Gee, that long, huh? Why don't you tell me all about it."

"You really want to know?" said Levan. He looked pleased.

"Oh, yes, yes indeed."

"Gee," he said. He lowered his boot away from my face and sat down in a nearby chair. "It all goes back to my childhood—"

"Come on, fellas," said Molly, busting in. "Chow's on!"

Thank God. I couldn't stand Levan's life story again. Molly? She was our jolly dimpled den mother. She had as much right to be a dirty old man as anyone. You heard of women's lib, right?

Clenched fists thrust into the air, we marched into the next room lustily shouting our battle song.

"Hi ho, hi ho!

"It's off to work we go!"

A huge white cake had been put in the center of the long banquet table. Red sugar roses and yellow scrolls covered its monumental sides. Molly smiled broadly. "How 'bout that?"

We sat down as the light dimmed and began spinning out colors and shimmering half-seen images.

"Blatt!" exploded a horn. My fur—I mean my hair—stood on end.

"Whaa, whaa!" it yowled.

"Good grief!" Freddy held his ears. "What's that?"

The music wailed like a maddened dog. Where? Where . . . my computerlike mind churned. "Ah ha! I remember now! That's classical stripper music!"

Horns burped twice. The cake quaked and the top sluffed off onto Levan. "@&$#!!" he said, struggling with the sticky stuff.

"TarRAAA!"

Up leaped Ginny-O. I didn't know her name then. Grinning widely, she scissored out onto the table. She was great, bumping and grinding like an old trooper, gobs of icing flinging off in all directions from her red-feather-covered gown.

A tear brimmed in Freddy's eye. "Gee," he whispered, "I always wanted to go to an old-fashioned Jaycees' meeting before I died."

She must have studied the old flicks, 'cause she was damn good. She twirled pointless tassels and shucked layer after layer of costume to our appreciative roars. It was too good to last.

It didn't. The door banged open. In walked Bidwell, the butler. The music died. "Gentlemen, I'm sorry to intrude. But I must inform you that a bust is in progress." There was muffled shouting and the distant pounding of feet.

"We gotta get outta here!" wailed Levan.

"If you'll follow me, gentlemen," the butler said mildly. He walked over to the elegant plastic wall paneling and touched a bracket. A section zipped back, revealing a hidden passageway. "The Essex House is proud that it provides complete service to its customers, whatever their needs."

The secret passage wound its way down through the guts of the hotel, through the kitchen and the laundry to the basement. There we entered a dank tunnel which burrowed through the hill that stood behind the building.

Bidwell stopped short of the exit. "I'm sorry, but I cannot take you any farther. We butlers are rather attached to our jobs, you know. Beyond here is the Cincinnati National Forest. You'll have a chance here."

Freddy scrambled to the tunnel entrance and peered around the corner. He scurried back. "Hey, Bidwell, when was this used last?"

The butler harrumphed. "I'll have you know, sir, we deal only with legitimate revolutionaries. Decent burners and pillagers don't come along every day."

"*Bidwell!*" said Freddy.

"Ahem. Not since the sex revolt, sir."

"That's better. You ought to keep up with things. There's an orgy going on in the mouth of your secret tunnel."

We made a run for it. Every man for himself. I grabbed our little stripper, tossed her on my shoulder, and followed the rest. There was a wild mélange of anachronistic costumes as clumsy medieval knights blundered through the Dionysian rites. I had impressions of bare-breasted women turning in surprise and men in togas shaking their fists. Then we were in the forest.

About a mile from the tunnel I slumped to earth gasping. The Teddi Bear outfit was pure hell. I couldn't sweat.

"Sorry, kid. I can't carry you another foot."

"I—I can walk now, I think." She was pretty. Brunette, dark small features. Tears streaked her dusty face.

We could hear the anguished whoop-whoop of sirens back by the hotel. There was an occasional *wap!* as a grabbolt caught someone. "What is your name?" Lordy, was I hot in that suit!

"Ginny-O." Her face brightened. "Are you Teddi Bear?"

I felt my face flush with shame. Thank heavens I was wearing a mask. Now she knew the truth about me. "Yeah," I said, feeling rotten.

"Oh, wow! Oh, wow! Can I have your autograph?" she whooped before I could shut her up.

They caught us two miles away. We awoke aboard the blue blimp the fuzz used, not knowing what hit us until we realized where we were. They got us with grabbolts.

It was during the long overnight flight to Washington that I developed the idea that led to the revolution. The old sexual underground held that human beings should be free to enjoy their bodies in whatever way they wanted. As long as others weren't exploited. When they took over, it became the law of the land.

All the freaks went overground. Except us poor dirty old men. They claimed we were exploiters. Now is that fair! They said everything was one way with us. That isn't true, never was!

Anyway, if we could use the Kaelson Process to develop the kids' sex organs, why, we'd be out from under the law. Great! Only, how could it be done?

With this in the back of my mind, I went before Judge Pollyester the next day. Boy! If he realized what would happen next, he'd never have let me go.

Ah, that was a good time. I was in my prime. I had wealth,

power. Millions of kids witnessed my feely programs, their sweet little heads encased in receptors. Yet I was unhappy. I was being watched. One slip in my ratings and I would be busted.

Worse, my immunity didn't spread to my friends. Freddy, Levan, the others at the Essex House fiasco, were getting their gray wrinkles smoothed in the Ohio State think and chem shop. I tried—man, how I tried—but I couldn't get them out.

I met Molly a month after we got back to Cincinnati in a small greasy spoon near the feely studios. "It's not fair," she stormed. One of her rare fits of anger. "They wouldn't believe I belonged to DOMpa."

I was unable to suppress a chuckle. "You mean they wouldn't bust you?"

"Yeah. And you watch it, wise guy. That's discrimination. I'll see my local."

I swallowed. You don't muck with women's lib. Especially the Ciny local. "Shh, people are staring at us."

"They wouldn't if you weren't wearing that silly fur suit," she snapped.

I quieted her down. Good thing she wasn't black too, Now that's a tough union, baby.

"It's going slow, Teddi," she said, "awfully slow. Every day I sit in the park watching likely recruits. We'll never rebuild our DOMpa cell at this rate. You just don't find dirty old men like you used to."

"Yeah," I said gruffly. "It's the passing of an era, a whole way of life. That's progress for you, though. Here, have some more wine."

"Don' mind if I do. Thanks. Anyway, I need money, lots of it."

"Money?" Unconsciously I clasped my wallet.

"Yeah, you old lovable tightwad. I want ta start a chain of candy stores."

"Candy stores? What's wrong with the super mark—" I stopped as the brilliance of the scheme hit me. I could see the ad: *Like children? Quarter Candy Stores has an opening for you.*

"Great, huh? How 'bout some more wine?"

"Sure, sure." I poured, then ordered another bottle.

The big break came unexpectedly. I was doing a show by the Sea of Tranquillity Industrial Park. Things were gloomy, the morning sun hadn't burned away the overnight smog yet. That week the show was supposed to be in the park. An educational thing—each day we would cover a different industry.

We were set up on a large ledge overlooking the sea of factories. Here and there red and sometimes blue light flashed among the squat buildings. It's exciting to see machines that are big, that go *bang!* and *pow!* and *do* something. Not like on Earth.

Earth was half full in the black sky, and I was jumpin' up and down, making with the yaks like a teddy bear should. But the program was dead. Like, nothing. The kids wouldn't open up and sparkle.

"Come on, Charlie," I said to one of the older boys. He was a blue-eyed ten-year-old with closely cropped yellow hair. "Give. Out with it. What's bugging you guys?"

"Gee, Teddi," he said, shoving his mitts deep into his spacesuit pockets. He kicked a pebble. I could sense that delicious feedback tingle you get when your audience is digging your show. This was big. "Haven't you heard? The dirty ol' hippie pigs took away our comic-smut."

I stood on my head, thumbing my nose at him. "Comic-smut?" The feedback tingle was growing.

"Yeah," said George-O, the Chink brat we had to give the show racial balance. He scampered out of the feely field, picked up a viewscreen from our pile of floater rafts and broadcasting equipment, and trundled it back. "Comic-smut,"

I muttered to myself. Alarms silently pulsed in my head. I bounced to my feet. This had bad vibes, but I let it ride. The feedback was too strong.

He flipped the set on. The kids' space helmets bumped as they pushed in close. I almost tossed my cookies as the war flick came on. It was damn good none of the kids could see my face beneath my fur-covered spacesuit. A sick, cold nausea gripped my guts.

This was pornography, the real uncut stuff. Bodies jumped and bounced as they were riddled with bullets. Women ran screaming, their clothes and hair on fire. And it was being broadcast into millions of homes too. Lord save me from Judge Pollyester now! It was the Ohio think and chem shop for me.

I reached to shut the set off. Something made me stop. I took a good look at the kids' eyes. Bright and shiny, like little nickels. They really dug that filth. I froze. Man, it's tough making a decision like that. I'd lose the kids if I shut it off. Lose them, and I was done. On the other hand, leave it on and I was helping to spread porn. And the judge'd get me.

I made the only decent and honorable decision a teddy bear could make. "Gee, gang," I said, "that's great stuff. Who said you can't watch it?"

"Judge Pollyester," said George-O, annoyed. "Can't you see we're watching?"

"Judge Pollyester?" I echoed, legs wobbly.

"Yeah." He spit in derision. The gob struck the inside of his helmet and ran down the plastic into his collar, to his irritation. The war flick was forgotten in the general merriment.

My mind clicked and spun like an old-fashioned adding machine. The feedback was zapping in like crazy. I shut off the outside mike. "Herbie, conjure Judge Pollyester for me, will you?"

"Now?" Herbie croaked, somewhere under the pile of broadcasting junk. "While we're on the air?"

"Yeah, yeah. Quick. Set him on the other side of the kids."

Herbie mumbled a curse. I could hear the *boop! boop! beep! bop!* as he buttoned the judge.

Pop! The polluted vacuum shimmered. A dark flicker, and a twelve-foot-high Judge Pollyester belched into existence. He glanced around, saw the kids' viewscreen, and scowled.

"You called," he boomed, shoving his hands into the sleeves of his black robe.

The kids shrieked, scrambling away from the huge figure.

"Christ, Herbie!" I howled, almost forgetting to change circuits, "shrink him down!"

Sell out? I mean this was my last chance. Turn the kids in before a billion people, make a point for law and order. It'd get the judge off my back. And get my fans on it. The thought reawakened my courage. I plunged bravely on.

"Har-har," I said. The judge's image wavered, shrank until it was knee high. "That cut him down to size!" That beautiful feedback—which had died when the judge appeared—came plowing in again.

Pollyester took a yellow flower from his long gray hair with a tiny hand and flicked it. The flower's image harmlessly passed through me. "You won't get away with this, you know."

I danced a bright little jig. "Get away with what, baby?"

"That comic-smut!" the small black figure exploded. "It's illegal, it's obscene, that's what. I'll have your hide for this!"

"Who said it's obscene?" I gestured at the viewscreen. I kept my eyes off the war flick to keep my stomach from heaving.

"I . . . that is, the court did. I mean, Congress passed the law. We said it's constitutional. You've had it!"

I shivered. Should have copped out. Damn! Why didn't I ever research things like I should? Too impulsive. Then I had it.

Oozing confidence, I laughed. "Now, Judge, tell me sincerely, what is wrong with that stuff? After all, it has a certain—though admittedly minor—redeeming social value. Why can't they watch it?" From the set I could hear the groaning and roaring of war machines and the whimpering of dying victims. "I mean, in this perfect world of ours—this place of freedom and free love—what drives them to watching comic-smut?"

Pollyester shook a tiny fist. "I couldn't care less what makes the little jerks and frustrates watch it. They're not going to, that's all!"

"Wanna bet?" I said sardonically. "Look, you called them jerks and frustrates, right?" The kids were watching me, the comic-smut forgotten. The feedback was juicin' in. "You know why they're frustrated, don't you? They can't have sex, that's why. It's everywhere—there's lovemaking in the streets, there's lovemaking in the parks, there's lovemaking at home.

"Straight love, gay love, every possible combination. Nothing's hidden, nothing's considered shameful. I admit this is good. This is peace, love. But what about the poor damn kids? How do they feel, always left out, watching from the sidelines. Did you ever feel sorry for them?"

"Arr—" said the judge. He was beaten. I could feel it. "There's nothing that can be done for them. It's too bad, but —"

"But you're wrong!" I cut in. I turned to the kids. "Gang, I happen to know the pigs right now have a man in the Ohio think and chem shop—having his brain smooth—who can give you sex, *real sex!*"

"Real sex?" said Charlie with awe and delight. "You mean we wouldn't have to play orgy, and like that. We could have real ones?"

"Gee," said Ginny-O, "we wouldn't have to fake rape, huh? Goshwow!"

"Yeah," I said gruffly.

George-O whooped. The whole bunch tried to talk at once, laughing and tumbling in the light lunar gravity. The comic-smut played on, forgotten.

The show was almost over. Quick tie it up. Pointing at the small image of Judge Pollyester, I said, "Kids, this is the man who won't let you have sex. What do you say about that, huh? Is he going to get away with that?"

"No!" thundered the studio gang. The feedback throbbed. God, I loved that feedback.

The little figure snarled at me. "It'll never work! You'll never get away with it, you dirty old man."

I laughed. "You know, kids," I said, addressing the feely audience, "if someone like the judge is bugging you, bug me. And I'll bug him right back. Just give me a call. Remember, bug Teddi Bear."

Boy, did I go into hiding fast. I had really stirred up an ant heap. Everybody joined in, both for and against kiddy sex.

Now let me get this straight. I didn't bug out, like some of my detractors claimed. No, sir! I did my share. But I had to hide. Now that's only common sense. I continued the Teddi Bear Show on the underground network. Let me tell you, that wasn't easy. We had to lug our equipment from one hidden studio to the next. One day we'd do the show from a poor medianstrip farmer's hut, using old fence wire on the dirt floor for a feely grid. The next, we'd hook onto the steel reinforcing rods in a concrete apartment building and broadcast from there.

The bug Teddi Bear calls became a big hit, until my victims got wise and hung up when I called.

See, I was very busy. Somebody had to stay in the rear and cheer the troops on. A mean, dangerous business. I was the revolution's symbol. I gave it strength with my broadcasts. Besides, I didn't want my ratings to slip.

In fact, I nearly got busted in a demonstration. It happened in Bloomington, a Chicago suburb. I knew we were in trouble the instant we got out of the air with the show.

"Geez, Herbie, what's that racket out there?" Garbled

chanting was coming through the thin walls of the old commune. "Do the fuzz know we're here?"

Herbie crawled from under his broadcasting equipment. He stood wiping his sweaty round face. "I dunno. Hell, it was all I could do to keep that racket from going out over the air."

Molly came out of the director's niche. "Don't get up tight. This is a scheduled demo."

I cursed. "What do you mean, scheduled? Who scheduled it?"

"DOMpa Central," she said reluctantly.

I groaned, smacking the fur on my forehead. "Don't they know we're doing a show here today? There must be cops everywhere by now!"

"Aw, be fair," she said. "You know we can't get computer time. We've got to do our own thinking."

Fuming, I walked into the next room, which had windows overlooking the twisting narrow streets of the tenement district.

"Two, four, six, eight!

"We want to fornicate!'

Thousands of singing, chanting kids marched below. They were naked, symbolically protesting the uselessness of their sex organs. Curbs were jammed with enraged adults snarling insults and threats. The privileged classes never learn. In the distance an evil red glow lit the early evening sky. There had been a contraceptive warehouse in that direction.

"We gotta blow this pad," I said as two blue blimps slid into view.

The street was jammed. The show's kids had stripped down and they joined the march. The three of us adults, clad in expensive plastic armor, carried our streetboards as we pushed through the mob on the sidewalk. This was a tough middle-class neighborhood and we were out of place. Dark creaking tenements hunkered up against the walks, creating an oppressive feeling. Through gaps in the crowd we could see the youthful marchers moving slowly in a direction opposite to ours.

To our dismay, the march bent around the next corner. We were boxed in. "Our pickup point is a mile away on the other side," whispered Molly. "We've got to get across."

How? Crawl through the sewers? Swing across on a rope? We didn't dare try crossing through the march. We were adults.

A couple of liberals took off their clothes and tried to join the parade. They came back reeling. "You dirty, loving hypocrites!" shouted the angry demonstrators. At the curb the liberals were beaten up by a half a dozen parents with wooden clubs.

"Why'd they kick those guys out of the march?" Molly protested.

"Because," said Herbie, "the kids know they're being hypocritical. It's all show. Sure, they'd march now. But when it's over they'd go home and make love, like everybody else."

I looked at Herbie in surprise. Simple round-faced Herbie. How militant he had become. "What should they do," I cracked, "castrate themselves?"

"Maybe," said Herbie thoughtfully. "Maybe they should."

"Weird," I snorted. This wasn't getting us out of there.

I sidled up to an eight-year-old girl who looked like a parade marshal and said, "Hsst, kid! The three of us gotta get across. Could we—" She glowered and kept on walking. "Look, the fuzz are after us. I—" No go. Desperately I whispered, "Keep this quiet. I'm Teddi Bear, and the cops are hot on us."

Her eyes narrowed. "Teddi Bear? Prove it." She kept walking.

Prove it? In front of everyone? "Look, would you believe it if I showed you I was wearing my fur outfit? I mean, just a little bit?"

She stopped and looked directly at me, starting to believe. I lifted up my chain mail until a patch of brown costume showed, hoping no one else would notice.

"Hey, look," shouted a man on the curb, "that little guy's taking his clothes off!"

"Shame! Shame!" howled the mob up and down the street. Shaken, I yanked my armor down. I had been noticed, but at least no one knew my real identity.

"Oooo, Teddi Bear!" whooped the little parade marshal.

I groaned. The adults shrieked and howled. I had only one choice. One way to go. "Hah-hah!" I shouted, ripping off my helmet. "Here's your own, lovable Teddi Bear!" Dropping my streetboard, I ducked from the mob and scampered in among the cheering kids.

Behind me were Molly and Herbie. Though I laughed, I felt twinges of unease as the parade restarted. The pickup point was also behind me. And getting farther away.

My duty to my fans came first. I sang, danced, and turned cartwheels. The blanking plastic armor hampered my movements and the scabbard kept flapping between my legs and tripping me. The stuff cost a pretty quarter—I wasn't about to throw it away. But after flopping on my face twice I gave in and took it off. Sylvy-O, the parade marshal, kept it for me. Ah, that was my style! I fairly flew, dancing and flipping somersaults without effort. Live performances are great.

As the evening lengthened, I started to worry. The march was a ball, but bedtime was coming up quick. That's the hell of it when you gotta depend on kids. Who would get me first, the enraged parents on the sidewalks or the fuzz overhead?

The clocks struck twenty-one. I felt a tugging at the fur on my arm. Sylvy-O stood there with my armor rolled up in a sack. "Gee, Mr. Teddi Bear, but I gotta go now."

"But kid, the demo—"

"I'm sorry, but I got school tomorrow."

With a sinking feeling I thanked her and took the bag. Here it comes. I've had it. Where could I hide? The protest was coming apart like wet cardboard. The waiting adults were becoming bolder. Already they were edging onto the street, eyes gleaming.

If only everyone left at once, maybe I could get away in

the confusion. "Hey, kids—" A smokebomb exploded. Suddenly I couldn't see. The air was filled with coughing and alarmed cries, I wiped my watering eyes, almost not hearing the dull clang behind me.

"What the—" I yelped. I felt a tugging at my leg. Powerful hands grasped my ankle. I was roughly yanked down into a hole in the street. Hands clamped my muzzle shut and I couldn't scream. There was another metallic clang overhead as I hit the bottom of the hole.

A light sprang on. I was down in the sewers of Bloomington, surrounded by friends. Molly, Freddy, kids from the show, even old Levan.

"Gee, am I glad to see you guys. Did Herbie get away too?" I stood up, dusting myself off.

"Dunno," said Molly. "He went off mumbling about castrating people and disappeared. We can't talk now, we gotta get out of here."

"Okay, let's go." Nobody moved. They were staring at me. Uneasily, I said, "What are we waiting for?"

"You've got to take off that Teddi Bear suit first," said Levan.

"W-what?"

"Yeah!" snapped Freddy. Gad, I had trusted that guy.

"Listen," said Molly, grabbing my arm, "that costume'll give us away."

"No!" They moved at me. I had thought they were my friends. A clang came from overhead. We froze. Another clang, and a metallic scraping. They were prying up the sewer cover. We turned and ran, the Teddi Bear suit forgotten.

We escaped Bloomington hidden under garbage in a sanitation department streetraft. The vehicle was stopped before it reached the local food reprocessing plant. We climbed out of our smelly quarters and continued south, concealed in a couple of Quarter Candy Store franchise streetrafts. The candy chain was big business now and had sales units everywhere. Damned convenient.

My success at Bloomington inspired DOMpa Central. It wanted me to appear everywhere. But I pointed out how lucky it was I hadn't been busted. Too risky. Reluctantly they agreed.

Herbie was gone. For a whole week I was frantic. I spent the time touring the ruins of Miami and the Florida Salt Desert, going out of my tree. At last DOMpa found me a replacement. They were good for something at least.

A month later Herbie popped up in New York, working for the Abstainers, a militant group of adult sympathizers. Their symbol was a chastity belt which was allegedly locked up for the duration. It was supposed to prove the purity of their motives. Herbie had been talked out of castrating everybody. The group grew quickly.

The idea was too kinky. Everybody started wearing chastity belts. But they weren't terribly chaste, and the Abstainers faded away. Before I could get to New York, Herbie disappeared again.

I missed Herbie. What had gotten into his head? His replacement was a dud. With the constant pressure of the show, I never had time to make a real search.

The Establishment got panicky. Judge Pollyester eased the ban on comic-smut. Cowboy flicks became legal. That didn't calm the uproar. He eased up again, allowing war movies and private dick stories. Finally, in desperation, he legalized Abbott and Costello.

To no avail. We grew stronger.

From the sunken shore of California to metropolitan New England, kids joined us. From the deserts of Florida to the uneasy frontier of South Dokotia, beyond which the Chinese People's Army roamed, we gathered strength. They were tired of being bedside spectators, tired of being the only deprived sector of society. They held sleep-ins in bordellos. Contraceptive outlets were blown up. Protesters went to orgies and stood around looking pathetic and glum.

At first teenagers were the staunchest supporters of the status quo. The newly rich usually are. We worked on them, forcing them to remember what it was like to be without the joys of sex. Slowly they came to our side. Thoughtful adults, noting the noise and violence of our movement, decided we must be right.

And we, we of DOMpa, chortled with secret glee. Soon, soon we would be victorious. Our vice would be legal. Soon it wouldn't be a proud but lonely thing to be a dirty old man.

Judge Pollyester was the black-cloaked symbol of reaction. He forgot about love and peace and shouted wild threats and vituperation. He searched through the forbidden archives of comic-smut, dredging up newsreels of Auschwitz and Doris Day–Rock Hudson flicks. To lure my audience he started his own show, The Big Teddy Bear Hunt. Wearing a Great White Hunter helmet, the judge ran around the country zapping anyone who looked like a teddy bear.

We countered. We offered code-o-graphs badges. Sets of the *Encyclopedia Erotica*. Secret periscope rings, which were complete with a tiny but usable set of wrenches, a saw, a hammer, a screwdriver, a flashing light suitable for sending Morse code, and a full-size full-color reproduction of the original Marilyn Monroe foldout nude.

But we were worried. There was a flaw in our scheme. Our best gimmick was the nude kiddy bit. Fall was approaching. It was getting cold outside.

We had to pull it off soon. Money to finance our operation kept pouring in from the Quarter Candy Store chain. Gee, I wish I had kept my stock in it.

But our biggest trouble was planning. If we'd had access to computers, I'm sure we'd never have depended so heavily on the nudity thing. That's the trouble. The Establishment always controls the computers, and you can't think of everything. Someday, when I get out, I think I'll go into the underground computer business.

October the eighth arrived. "How is it out there?" I said,

peeping out of my sleeping bag. This was it, the day. Freddy walked across the tent and poured hot water into the plastic basin. "Cool, nice," he said, scrubbing his face briskly.

I crawled out of the sack, went outside. There was still frost on the grass, but it would be warm.

"We can't get the kids out," said Molly, coming from the HQ. "Leastways not naked."

I shrugged. "We'll have to wait. Can't really push them now, you know." I put my arm around her wide waist, and we walked to the chow tent. It was scary. We had to make it now, there'd be no second chance. She put her arm around me. She felt it too.

The night before, the kids had roamed unmolested through the streets and yards of the suburbs surrounding Washington. The terrified adults had remained barricaded in their apartments. This wasn't the first revolutionary army that passed this way.

After breakfast the air warmed quickly. The kids stripped down to their skin, mounted their streetboards carrying their flags and signs. Hundreds of thousands of them. This was it.

I looked at the strained faces in the banks of viewscreens. The tension was unbearable. Coordinators and feely techs hustled frantically around me in the hidden HQ. I felt a little more confident. This was the first revolt of the feely generation. The Establishment was in for a surprise.

Sector after sector reported in. Good thing I had let the troops have recess a few minutes before. Now they were combat ready.

The last report. I looked at my friends around the room. Good bunch, I thought warmly. Would we still be together tomorrow at this time? Molly, Freddy, the kids, and that old goat Levan. I wished Herbie was standing there with us. Somehow it didn't seem right without him. I gave the word—

—The feely techs spun their dials like fiends. The even ranks of kids moved. Suddenly the lines broke up into a wild melee, with kids running in every direction, jumping into rolling, tumbling piles. Almost as suddenly, it was over. Only now, by the magic of feely, our army had been multiplied by a factor of twenty. Let the Establishment figure this one out!

What we had done was simple, of course. The concrete streets of the city were strengthened with iron reinforcing bars. We had hooked onto them, creating a giant feely field. Our horde charged into the city and the waiting blue meanies.

"Two, four, six, eight!

"We want to fornicate!"

"Gee," said Ginny-O. "Our strength is the strength of twenty, for our hearts are pure!"

I winced. "Back to your salt mine, kid."

She clicked her heels and saluted. Then limped off to the message board.

Washington, D.C., is a square city. We came at it from all four sides. Those coming in from Arlington were diversionary. They would be bottled up by the bridges over the Potomac. Same with those coming out of the southeast, though there were more bridges over the Anacostia. We couldn't leave the highways and cross the water on our streetboards, because we'd be out of range of the feely fields. We'd lose our doppelgangers.

Grabbolts flashed into the sky, roving back and forth uselessly. They were unable to differentiate between the kids and their duplicates. We got a mile and a half into the city before the fuzz figured out what we were doing. A sudden surge of countering current flashed through the reinforcing rods. They didn't have our code sequence. The images didn't even flicker. We exhaled with relief. We had been dreading this, and we had come through in great shape.

One by one the grabbolts scored lucky hits. They wouldn't even slow us down at this rate. We were beginning to get cocky in the HQ.

"Hey, guys," I said, "can you picture a teddy bear running for President?"

Freddy and Levan made a show of groaning. I shut up.

But I wasn't ready to put the idea out of my mind. After all, this was going out over the underground network.

Our southeastern salient, sliding up the ancient Suitland Parkway, ran into a solid wall of fuzz at the Anacostia. It stopped dead. Moments later our southwestern army hit the fuzz at the Potomac. Desperately, we tried to confuse the meanies by pouring images through their lines. It didn't work.

Our northern units had better luck. They plowed into the cops at U Street. This time the image worked. The bewildered cops fell back, re-forming on Massachusetts Avenue. There they held.

An army that isn't going forward is in trouble. That was us. For the next ten minutes we tried everything. Direct frontal assault with masses of kids. They bounced. We tried the sewers. No go. Anyone who got through was zapped by the long arm of the Establishment.

It was falling apart. "Hey," I said, grabbing Levan by the arm, "get a bunch of DOMpa guys. They're big enough to shove their way—"

A shout of dismay came from the viewscreens. "Ooh, Teddi," Ginny-O yelped, "quickly, *quickly!*"

"Damn!" I said. "Wait here." I patted old Levan on the back, then hurried to the commotion, grumbling to myself. Did I have to do everything?

The sight on the screen jolted me. There, like a black-robed King Kong, stood Judge Pollyester. One hand rested on the Washington Monument, as though it was a walking stick. The other held a huge red banner which was mounted on a pole.

You Shall Undercome! it read.

The giant stirred. With two-hundred-foot-long strides he lumbered east on Constitution. Our northern army panicked. Up and down the line whole groups broke and ran. Some of the doppelgangers began to fade as feely techs let fear stiffen their fingers.

"Hey, you schmucks!' I shouted, banging on my desk, "stay with it!"

"Oh," wailed Molly, "we've lost! We've lost!"

I looked at the chaos spreading through the room. People were milling around aimlessly, faces frozen with shock. Messengers clasping undelivered notes stared at the screens where grabbolts were striking with increasing accuracy. Damn those techs! Once the doubles faded, the kids were sitting ducks. Strangers were running in and out of the HQ spreading panic. If I didn't reassert authority immediately, the whole thing was going to blow up. I had to be forceful. Now.

"Hey, Teddi, where're you going?" said Molly.

"Ah . . . well . . . I thought I'd step out for a cup of coffee and a bite to eat. Why don't you keep track of things. I'll be back in an hour or— Say, what're you doing? Let me down!" Hands grabbed me.

"No you don't, Teddi Bear. You're going to burn here with us," said Freddy.

"Yeah," whined Levan. You got us into this. Now get us out."

I snorted. Lord, I was in trouble! This had to be carried off good. What's your problem? Just tell 'em the giant is a feely image. It can't hurt them. Do I have to do everything?"

I had carried it off. They lowered me to my feet. Nevertheless, I had the distinct feeling I was being escorted when I returned to the screens.

It was a rout, a complete rout. We no longer had an army, we had a terrified mob reeling back in retreat. The blue grabbolts methodically worked them over, chewing great holes in their shattered ranks.

In spite of my brave show I was sweating. I grabbed the mike. "Now listen here, baby. That there judge is just doing a big supersized feely schtick. Pay no heed!"

I could have been speaking to the wind. The wild retreat

went on. "Heh, heh," I said. A— Do ya mind? I'll be right back. I gotta go on pisscall." Hands grabbed me.

What to do? My buddies, my pals, had an unfriendly look in their eyes. I wracked my brain. An image of a teddy bear, a tear in its glass eye, its stuffing scattered across the floor, came to mind. Gee, I had a real stake in this too. If the revolt collapsed, the underground feely net would disappear. Not only that, but now I wouldn't be able to get back on the Establishment nets. Oh, wow!

Wait a minute. If Judge Pollyester could go giant economy size, so could I.

Though I was in the studio, to my senses I was standing—well, towering Godzilla-like above the concrete. I was on old I-95, at the Arlington county line. Ahead, the ancient highway carved its way into the city. The rice paddy terraces on its shoulders were barren dollops of brown mud now that the harvests were in.

In the distance, looming Rodin-like over the buildings, I could see the black shape of Judge Pollyester chasing our army. "Scat, scat!" he croaked, stomping on the pavement.

I cupped my hands. "Hey, you bird-brained lummox! Why don't you pick on someone your own size!" Priceless window glass shattered all around me. "Geeze," I said, switching circuits momentarily, "turn the volume down."

The judge swiveled. "Aha, Teddi Bear. So we meet again!" he said, with gusto. "This is the end, you know. You're finished."

I laughed. "You're wrong, Judge. Youth and justice always win out in the end. Don't you ever watch comic-smut?"

With rapid strides I headed into the city. I was on the air again, getting that old feedback tingle. It was great.

Just south of Arlington National Cemetery I came upon our retreating troops. "Hey, kids, it's me, your old hero, Teddi Bear," I boomed. More glass shattered.

They shrieked and dove off the highway instead of rallying.

The last of their feely doubles vanished. My huge size had scared them. I got down on my hands and knees. "Consarn you, you little beggars, get back there and fight like—well, fight."

But they were gone. Grumbling, I climbed to my feet and headed toward the Potomac.

"*You nerd!*" said Molly over the internal circuit. She cursed fluently. "You almost gave away the whole show. Don't make anymore unprogrammed moves like that."

I swallowed hard, made a quick apology. No one else knew how close we had come to disaster. My knees felt wobbly. The feedback grew in power.

The judge was waiting for me at the corner of Seventeenth and Constitution. He poked at me with his pole.

I sneered. "You can't touch me with that, you schmuck. Don't you know that?" The feedback was throbbing. This was it, the confrontation. My audience was sopping it up. This was my element, and I was glorying in it.

"Of course I know that," he snapped. "Oooh, do I wish I could, though. I'd twist you into a pretzel!"

"Tut tut, cut out that comic-smut violence. This's a family show." It had to be done quickly. I walked straight at Polly-ester. I slid through his image without resistance.

He snorted. "What are you up to? You know you have to be here in person."

Ignoring him, I took a few quick steps to the edge of the White House lawn. From out of my image's belly plunged a stolen blue blimp. The cabin doors flipped open and out dropped a dozen figures sitting crosslegged on streetboards.

For precious seconds the White House guards, scattered across the grass, stood and gaped. The squad of kids, Molly in the lead, hurtled down at an angle. Belatedly, blue grab-bolts flashed into the air. Too late. The small group smashed through the second-floor window and was gone from sight.

One minute. Two minutes. I forced an exhale. What was going on in there? The tension squeezed me. Then Molly's voice boomed out over the internal circuit. "We've got it! We've occupied the President's office. Hell, this was easier than taking over a university!"

Judge Pollyester made a stricken sound.

The feedback roared. I reeled under its fantastic power, almost getting my jollies right there. "Tough lucksky, Judge baby. Out with the corrupt old order. In with the new."

"What, the corrupt *new* order?"

"Tush, tush, don't be bitter."

He shook his fist at me. "Curse you, brown Teddi Bear!" His image winked out.

Chuckling, I addressed the millions out there who had watched our little bit of revolutionary street theater. "Well, kids, we've shown those bourgeois hippie pigs a thing or two—"

"Stop it, Teddi," said a familiar voice. I spun.

"Herbie!" His pudgy figure loomed Mighty Joe Young-like above Pennsylvania Avenue. "What're you doing here?"

"You're a hypocrite, Teddi. You don't believe in the revolution. You're using it for your own evil purposes." His eyes seemed glazed.

He lumbered toward me, drawing a knife. An electric chill went through me before I remembered he was only a feely image.

My courage came back. "What're you going to do, castrate me so I can be a true believer?" I danced a little jig. "Don't you know us teddy bears have nothing to lose?"

"Who cares," he said grimly. "You've dishonored that Teddi Bear suit, and I'm going to take it from you."

He reached out and grabbed me. He was solid! My head swirled. A new feely development? Then came the stunning, sickening realization. He was with me back in the studio.

"No," I breathed, trying to pull away. Before the whole world, I lost my Teddi Bear suit.

Oh, the humiliation. I, the handsome, virile masked Teddi Bear of the kiddy hours, exposed—shown to be a mere human being. How dreadful! I went into seclusion, hoping someday this would be forgotten and I could once more hold my head high.

The next day I received an offer from my former employers, and they wouldn't take no for an answer. That night I was back with the old Teddi Bear Show. Ahem, with a suitable raise, since I was now a successful revolutionary.

Ah yes, the revolution was a success. A reluctant Congress passed the necessary laws. The Kaelson Process was made legal for one and all. And that is how the harsh and repressive Hippie Era ended and how the benevolent Teddi Bear Age began.

But my own saga didn't end as happily, as you know. Revolutions have a well-known tendency to swallow their own. The bleakness of my fate wasn't apparent immediately.

My show kids, the revolutionary cadre, were among the first to undergo the selective maturation process. It took over a month to complete the treatment. I went to the hospital the morning Ginny-O was to be released.

"Good grief!" I said, startled, as I walked into the waiting room. Judge Pollyester was there too. What did he want?

"Oh, this is a bitter moment, Teddi," he said. "It's still hard for me to believe you won."

"Friends?" I said, grinning.

He made a halfhearted attempt to smile. I could afford to be magnanimous; I was on top. I clapped him on the back and squatted on the cushions next to him. "How come you're still wearing your robes? I thought we got you kicked out of your job." It was impossible to resist a gentle needle.

"Eh, I'm sort of used to them. I feel funny wearing pants."

I was still puzzled. "What're you doing here? I thought you were against this whole idea."

He managed to smile weakly. "Well, I'm in charge of the maturation program. Heh, heh. Being a member of the Establishment has its privileges. The more things change, the more they remain the same, you know."

I felt a sudden revelation. Those who fight the hardest

against a vice often have repressed desires for that very thing. No wonder he hated us so.

We turned as the nurse led Ginny-O into the room. That's when it all fell apart.

Her movements were tentative—like a doe's—but vibrantly sexual. I heard the judge suck in his breath. My eyes were on Ginny-O. Her face had changed subtly. So had her hips. They were wide, a woman's hips. My arms trembled. Her breasts were pressed tightly by her blouse, which hadn't been designed to contain them, and the nipples showed.

I screamed and screamed as they led me away. The error in my schemes was too clear. I dug kids. Unfortunately, Ginny-O was now a miniature adult.

It's easy in retrospect to point out this was the obvious result of our plot. Don't forget we were dreamers. We thought we could get exactly what we wanted, and no more. Certainly, we weren't the first in history to have that delusion.

Ah, if only that'd been the extent of my misfortunes, I suppose I could have managed. Supreme irony! The kids quickly forgot my show after they underwent the Kaelson Process. I didn't join the swing to kiddy-sex programs that now caught their eye. As I told Herbie when he went at me with that knife, a teddy bear has nothing to lose. And I refused to change my costume.

Week after week my ratings dwindled. At last my show was canceled. It was then, when I'd sunk into obscurity, that the wolves of the old Establishment leaped on me. Ex-Judge Pollyester led the pack. Soon I was consigned to the Ohio think and chem shop.

They railroaded me. No one noticed, no one took my side. A sad, sad fate. I fought and raged, but it was no use. Pollyester plied his evil sense of poetic justice on me. Through the Kaelson Process I was reduced to the physical state of a normal prerevolutionary child.

"It's for therapeutic reasons," he cackled gleefully, rubbing his hands together. "You've got to learn how to be a proper child before you can become a proper adult."

The weight of my past sins gave him the leverage to do as he wanted. And none of my old fans came to my aid. Oh, it was awful. He had the court make me his ward, allegedly so he could keep an eye on me. There was nothing I could do. I'm trapped in a nightmare.

So now I'm his child, by adoption, and I—excuse me, that's Ginny-O calling me now.

"Coming, Mother!"

THOMAS BRAND

Don Slow and His Electric Girl Getter

When we last left Don Slow, youthful All-American genius, boy inventor, original young man from Racine, he had just created his greatest invention, his electric Girl Getter.

Actually, he had not intended to invent a Girl Getter at all. He intended to invent a death ray. Somehow, however, the electronic circuitry had gotten reversed and the results were exactly the opposite.

Don Slow discovered this fact for himself the very first time he aimed his new invention at a cage full of white rats and squeezed the trigger (stifling a really horrible giggle as he did so).

To his amazement, the rats did not keel over. Not at all. The rats squealed and jumped in the air and looked at each other with strange fiery looks. Squeaking at the top of their ratty lungs, they ran around in ratty circles, making out wildly in various ratty ways, until the inside of the cage looked like a fuzzy white pinwheel.

"That's odd," said Don Slow.

He studied his new invention curiously. Certainly it looked formidable enough to the untutored eye. It looked like a common ordinary household disintegrator laser beam ray gun.

Still, the full implications of his new invention did not immediately penetrate Don Slow's manly brow (not for nothing was he named Don Slow). It was not until much later in the day that Don Slow accidentally shot a beam from his ray gun into the parakeet cage.

The parakeet gave a Tarzan screech and kicked the door off. The parakeet roared out a window and into the blue, in soaring, lustful pursuit of eagles and hawks. (Some feathers from a well-ravaged condor were found later scattered over certain high passes in the Andes.)

Dawn broke slowly over the eastern horizon. "My goodness me," said Don Slow. "I have invented a nasty thingums."

Don Slow stood silent amid the smokings and stinkings within his Secret Laboratory contemplating his new invention. A strange gleam came to his eyes.

"We must experiment further," Don Slow told himself. "We must put this new device to the ultimate test."

Don Slow strode from his Secret Laboratory into his bedroom. He changed quickly from his laboratory clothes to his Don Slow costume with the jagged lightning bolt pointing toward his crotch. He put on his black mask.

Then Don Slow exited through a secret panel in the rear of the clothes closet. He went down a narrow passage built within the walls of the apartment house. He entered a secret chamber in a supposedly abandoned sewage disposal plant. Inside, a gleaming length of polished black machine was parked: Don Slow's most famous invention, RobotCar.

RobotCar was Don Slow's Faithful Servant and Loyal Sidekick. It was also his car. Don Slow had invented it during his Black Period. In addition to all its standard equipment, laser beams fore and aft, smoke screens, ejector seats, retractable beds with satin sheets, champagne dispensers and the like, RobotCar had a computer brain beneath its dashboard. The brain was programmed to communicate by electronic voice through the dashboard, issuing late reports on road conditions, pithy commentaries on passing scenery, reciting certain limericks, and uttering uplifting passages from Horatio Alger stories during moments of creative lassitude.

"Look, RobotCar," said Don Slow. "My latest and greatest invention."

"What the hell is that?" said RobotCar succinctly.

"It is my new electric Girl Getter. It is much the best thing that I have ever done. It is much better than my Ravishable Robot or my Submarine Sexlab. When I turn this ray gun on any girl of my choice, it will immediately defrost her and put her in an exceedingly susceptible mood. It will turn her on, RobotCar, it will really turn her on! More, my Faithful Servant and Loyal Sidekick, it will turn her into a raging, twitching, and dribbling sex fiend, intent only on attack and the immediate satisfaction of her irresistible urges. No one will be safe from her when this weapon is used, least of all me. I hope."

"It may be your greatest invention and it may not, Honorable Master," said RobotCar. "After all, it has yet to be proven in practice."

"Precisely why I am here," said Don Slow.

Don Slow slid into RobotCar's front seat. RobotCar's headlights gushed onto a wall of brick before them. Don Slow pressed a button and a section of the wall rose automatically. As the gleaming RobotCar swung out onto a deserted side street in an obscure section of town, the wall shut down behind. Buzzing like a gigantic insect, the sleek superpowered RobotCar roared out into the afternoon.

"We're off to hunt the biggest of all game," said Don Slow. "Broads!"

At that very moment, many blocks away, Sandra Smith, girl succulent morsel, stretched, yawned, and rose from her wall-to-wall mink-covered bed. As half a dozen maids sprang to her assistance, Sandra viewed herself in her wall-to-wall ceiling mirror. What she saw was so appetizing it even turned her on: vast elf eyes, waist-length platinum blond hair, ripe cherry lips. Sandra went ape eying her own 42-22-37 reflection.

Sandra was the Best of Breed. The best-looking, best paid, most successful poule de luxe in Space City, sought after even by people to whom her name was only a legend, a bright thrilling legend whispered in delicious gossip. Her techniques, her mastery of prolonged erotic torments, had made her the standard by which all others were measured, whether one was referring to calisthenics, bondage, trapeze acts, or simple ordinary everyday banging.

Her servant girls now went to work on Sandra, bathing her and scrubbing her until she glowed and tingled, brushing out her long platinum blond hair to a breathtaking silkiness, preparing her for her daily foray.

Clad in gleaming thigh-length boots, Sandra promenaded through her apartment, high heels clicking like ice in a glass.

Sandra exited through a secret panel in the rear of her clothes closet, which was hung with silks and satins, lavish furs, rubber skin suits, whips and lashes of various lengths and pliabilities. She went down a narrow passage built within the walls of her apartment house. She entered a secret chamber in a supposedly abandoned sewage disposal plant. Inside, a gleaming length of golden convertible was parked: Sandra's famous sportscar, Goldhump.

Goldhump was Sandra's trademark. The body of the convertible was sheathed in gleaming platinum, matching Sandra's own platinum blond mane. She cruised the boulevards and concourses in Goldhump, and everyone who saw her knew who was in that car and what she was after.

Sandra got in. Goldhump's headlights gushed onto a brick wall in front of them. Sandra pressed a button and a section of the wall rose automatically. As the gleaming sportscar swung out onto a deserted side street in an obscure section of town, the wall shut down behind. Purring like a gigantic pussycat, the sleek superpowered Goldhump roared out into the afternoon.

"I'm off to hunt the biggest of all game," said Sandra. "Kicks."

As they drove downtown, RobotCar recited several of Don Slow's favorite limericks, the one about the young man named Tobias, the one about the man from St. Clair, the one about the young girl made of glass.

Don Slow paid no attention. He was itching to try his new invention.

The streets seemed strangely empty. There were hardly any girls to be seen. There was, come to think of it, hardly anybody to be seen. Many of the stores and shops were closed.

"Where the hell is everybody?" demanded Don Slow.

"You know what?" said RobotCar. "My computer memory has suddenly come up with a fact. Today is the day of the big Time Circus parade."

Don Slow clapped his hand to his forehead. "Of course! That's where everybody is! Down at the Central Concourse watching the Time Circus parade. *That's* where we'll find the action!"

Goldhump purred through the streets of the city.

Sandra was puzzled. There were hardly any pedestrians around. There were plenty of her competitors around, but hardly anybody else.

She waved to her competitors (all mini-chastity belts and teased beehive hairdos). Her competitors, she noted with satisfaction, were forced to prowl the streets in mere Rolls Royces, Mercedeses, and Jags. Nothing as ornately status-making as Goldhump. Her competitors waved back or offered upraised middle fingers, depending on their degree of jealousy. Some of them spat.

The lack of customers puzzled Sandra.

Sandra parked at the curb by a sidewalk cafe where one of her Sisterhood sat noticeably alone in a sea of tables. "What are you doing. Sandra? Poaching on my territory?"

"Where is everybody?"

"They must all be down at the Central Concourse, watching the Time Circus parade."

Sandra hit her forehead.

"Of course! The Time Circus parade. *That's* where everybody is!"

The Time Circus was the biggest thing that had ever happened in Space City. The First Earth Expedition Back into Prehistoric Time had returned from its first trip through the world's first time machine with a host of captured specimens: dinosaurs and prehistoric beasties, and even some authentic ancient cavemen, Cro-Magnons and Neanderthals and the like. The specimens were being marched up the Central Concourse like an old-time circus parade with bands playing and banners flying.

Almost the entire population of Space City had turned out to watch the parade. It was a grand occasion. The great monsters came right down the center of the street, marching with ponderous tread, tyrannosauruses and brontosauruses and stegosauruses all with evil glints in their reptilian eyes, not big balloons, or moving imitations, but the real live thing, hissing and defecating in all directions.

Don Slow parked on a thronged side street where he could see the heads of the creatures promenading past. Don Slow was not watching the creatures. Don Slow was watching the creatures who were watching the creatures, the edible confections of redhead, brunette, and blonde who crowded the sidewalks in delicious swarms ooing and ahing at Cro-Magnon biceps.

An unplucked teenybopper with great green eyes stopped in front of RobotCar.

"Ooo, what a groovy car," she said, running her fingers over RobotCar's hood.

"Scat!" said RobotCar. "And get your sticky fingers off my self-polishing chrome. We're looking for bigger game."

"Come on," said a friend of the bopper's. "Never mind that car. We're missing the parade. Look! The saber-toothed tigers are going by."

"We can do better than *that,*" said RobotCar.

A murmur rose from the crowd. "Look, here come the woolly mammoths!"

Here indeed came a procession of woolly mammoths, marching ponderously end to end, woolly trunks grasping woolly tails. They were being prodded forward by Cro-Magnons wielding clubs. Even at this distance one could tell that the authenticity of the Cro-Magnons was unsullied by deodorants.

Don Slow viewed the spectacle with distaste. Yellow Cro-Magnon incisors did nothing for him.

Then all of a sudden through a break in their ranks Don Slow caught sight of a glimmering vision on the far side of the Central Concourse. A platinum blond vision, standing up on the front seat of a . . . a . . . could that be a platinum blond convertible?

The vision was so gleaming, so lustrous, that on the instant Don Slow entered it into a private and expansive niche in his fantasy life.

"Gee whillikers gosh, *look!*" said Don Slow.

RobotCar's antennas shot straight up in the air.

"Oh, yes, Honorable Master, I see it, I see it!" said RobotCar.

"She's it!" said Don Slow.

Don Slow unholstered his ray gun. "I am readying my irresistible Girl Getter." he said. "Prepare to move in."

Don Slow aimed across the parade route, centering the shining vision in his sights, steadying his wrist with his free hand.

Unfortunately for the public safety of Space City, Sandra Smith chose that exact moment to sit down. Don Slow followed her with his sights, and squeezed the trigger, bzzzzzt, as Sandra slid behind Goldhump's windshield.

The ray gave Sandra only a glancing blow off her sleek golden head, but it hit the angled reflecting surface of Goldhump's windshield with all full force and magnitude, splattering, *sproiinngg!* in all directions, bathing the circus parade, the Cro-Magnons, the woolly mammoths, and all the dinosaurs with democratic impartiality.

"Ooo," said all the spectators in appreciative chorus as they watched the electronic beam pass over their heads like a Fourth of July firepiece.

"Aaaa!" said all the spectators in chorus as the stampede started.

Dinosaurs roared. Woolly mammoths trumpeted. Multitudes scattered.

"Oh-oh," said Don Slow.

"You friggin' idiot," said RobotCar.

"Oh, my goodness," said Don Slow. He stood rooted in awe, staring, as the fruits of his folly manifested themselves.

Screamings and shriekings.

Shuddering with ecstasy, woolly mammoths collapsed on their woolly haunches, trumpeting cries of woolly mammoth bliss and spraying the street with jets of woolly mammoth sperm, like fireboats saluting a new arrival in the harbor.

More screamings and shriekings.

"I think perhaps we should leave," said Don Slow.

An avalanche of Cro-Magnon females, all incisors and pendulous dugs and wafting vapor trails, stampeded into the premises of the Pink Flit, an oh-so-charmingly decorated cocktail lounge frequented by delicate young men.

Screamings and shriekings you wouldn't believe.

"I *know* we should leave," said Don Slow.

"Look!" said RobotCar.

Across the Central Concourse, one of the woolly mammoths, rolling about in the throes of unutterable woolly mammoth rapture, was bearing down on Goldhump and its platinum blond occupant like a vast woolly bowling ball.

Goldhump's golden occupant shrieked a golden shriek as the woolly mammoth raised one giant woolly foot over her.

"To the rescue!" said Don Slow.

RobotCar spurred himself forward with his accelerator and extended a retractable arm, grasping Sandra in a retractable claw, hoisting her up by the nape of the neck, and plucking her out of Harm's Way a Scant Hairsbreadth before the descending woolly foot pulverized Goldhump into a pile of glittering golden junk.

"Eeeek," said Sandra as she was tossed into RobotCar's back seat all in a heap.

"Hi ho, RobotCar, awaaay," yelled Don Slow triumphantly.

RobotCar took the first corner on two wheels, snarling up an expansive boulevard, the advance guard of a general retrograde movement of unparalleled dimensions.

"My new invention!" exulted Don Slow. "It's a success—a success!"

"It sure is," said RobotCar. "That concourse is going to be dripping elephant come for a week."

"Where am I?" asked Sandra.

"You are safe in the hands of me, Don Slow, boy genius."

"I feel so funny," said Sandra. "I often get hot, but this is like . . . wild."

"It is all because of my new invention. You have been hit by my new superstimulating Girl Getter ray gun. In a few seconds you will attack me."

"Sonny boy, if I were going to attack you, you wouldn't have to send up smoke signals. You'd have got the message by now."

"Hmm, perhaps I didn't give you enough of a jolt."

Sandra had turned her attention to RobotCar's glittering interior.

"What an interesting car. So very plush. This is the first time I've ever seen a bidet in a back seat."

"My Honorable Master is extremely fastidious," said RobotCar.

"And what are all these little goodies, these odds and ends?" asked Sandra.

"They are all inventions of my Honorable Master," said RobotCar.

"Some of them are concave and some are convex. They all seem rather obvious."

"My Honorable Master designed them for self-entertainment during dull moments."

Don Slow said, "They are part of an extended experiment of mine where I am developing a mathematical relationship between certain simple pleasures and the flux of pure movement in both constant and accelerated states."

"How interesting," purred Sandra. Her eyes shone with the luminosity that registered discovery of a new kick. "How do they work?"

"Automatically. They are hooked up to RobotCar's power supply."

"Be careful how you handle those," said RobotCar, "I'm very sensitive there!"

"And, ah, where is the starting button on these little frizmicks?" asked she of the rising appetites.

"There isn't any," said Don Slow. "They are activated by voice request. You have merely to requisition services from RobotCar to inaugurate activities."

"Do you mind?"

"Not at all. We shall soon be at my Secret Laboratory, where I, Don Slow, boy genius, shall have my innings."

"RobotCar, do you mind?" purred Sandra.

"Oh, not at all, Fair Damosel, not at all," quavered RobotCar.

"Well, then, RobotCar, would you please serve me?"

"With everything at my disposal, Fair Damosel, with all my plugs and firing pins."

"Ah, RobotCar, that feels good," said Sandra. "That feels so very good."

"Watch it there, Faithful Servant and Loyal Sidekick," said Don Slow. "Don't get carried away with yourself. You're just a machine."

"Oh, oh, oh," moaned Sandra. "Oh, RobotCar, you know how to make a girl feel good. Oh, my darling RobotCar. Oh, my *dar*ling, *dear*est, Robot*Carrr!*"

"Oh, this is the way to go," said RobotCar. "This really cleans the carbon off the old plugs!"

"Oh, Ape Diddely," said Don Slow.

"I do believe you're jealous there, Dead Eye Dick," said RobotCar.

"Just keep your sensors on the road and don't hit anything!"

RobotCar was now sweeping with impressive speed toward a barrier of toll booths in the road. Cars blocked every Exact Change lane in front of them.

RobotCar swept through the Change and Receipt lane. Don Slow heard the spurned toll taker shout, then there were sirens, alarums, and excursions from the rear, and all the neon signs above the toll booths blinking

TILT

TILT

TILT

as RobotCar vanished up the highway.

"Oh, you're right," Sandra sighed. "Pleasure coupled with movement is just the kickiest."

A warning signal blinked redly on the dashboard: "Fuzz approaching. Fuzz approaching."

It was true. Fuzz *were* approaching. Don Slow could see their blips growing ominously on RobotCar's rear radar screen.

"We shall have to deal with these fuzz," said RobotCar.

"*You* deal with them," said Don Slow. "You're the one who went through the toll booths without paying."

"Oh, how yummy I feel," said Sandra.

"Shall I use my strange powers to cloud men's minds?" said RobotCar.

"*Anything!* Just get rid of them!"

"Oh, yummy, yummy, yummy."

"Drive faster, RobotCar! *You* can outrun those creeps!"

"I can't go faster! She's draining my batteries!"

"Oh, yummy burgers with ketchup on them!"

"Turn left at this next intersection!" ordered Don Slow. "Maybe we can shake them off our trail."

RobotCar screeched around the corner on two wheels.

"Oh, shit!" said RobotCar.

"RobotCar! You know better than to use language like that in front of a lady!" said Don Slow.

"It's this road you had me turn onto. It's the expressway! It's taking us straight back downtown to the Central Concourse!"

"Oh, shit," said Don Slow.

"And those fuzz are still hot on our trail too," said RobotCar.

Don Slow looked back. He could see them in person now. A pair of mounted cycle fuzz, growing larger by the second as they closed in on RobotCar's overtaxed self.

"Battle stations!" ordered Don Slow. "Prepare to repel boarders!"

One of the cycle fuzz, his buzzer blaring, now tried to sweep past them on the left, motioning for them to pull over. RobotCar stuck out an exhaust pipe. The fuzz went down like somebody'd picked him up for a spare.

"One down!" said Don Slow. He reached for a weapon, preferably his Stungun. He grabbed his Girl Getter. He drew a bead on the other approaching cycle fuzz.

"Look out!" said RobotCar, simultaneously slamming on all his braking systems.

The road just ahead was suddenly full of an onrushing mass of haunted-looking refugees, fleeing the downtown debacle.

"Zowiiieee!" said Sandra as she surged forward.

"Oops!" said Don Slow, firing his weapon.

This time he not only hosed down the entire street but included the nearby Municipal Museum of Antiquities and Egyptology in his awful field of fire.

"Ho, boy," said RobotCar. "I can feel this one coming."

As they watched, the doors to the museum burst from their hinges. A swarm of hideous linen-clad mummies poured out, some loping, some stalking, all bearing their mummified manhood before them like battering rams.

Universal screamings and shriekings.

The pursuing cycle fuzz screeched to a stop. He dismounted and fired a warning shot in the air. Then he turned and bolted like a deer. He and a mummy passed off RobotCar's stern together like a double shot from a Roman candle.

RobotCar roared back up the road in the direction whence they had come in Full Speed Reverse.

"Did you see that?" yelled Don Slow. "Did you see *that?* My new invention has restorative, rejuvenative, and resurrective powers!"

"All three of which you are going to need if any of those poor bastards back there ever catch up with us."

"We must tell the world!"

"The world is finding out, take my word for it, the world's finding out!"

"Your Honorable Master seems to have created something of a disturbance, RobotCar," Sandra observed brilliantly.

"My Honorable Master is an honorable asshole," said RobotCar.

"Knock it off, my Faithful Servant and Loyal Sidekick."

"Let me tell you, that's going to be some scene when those mummies tangle with those woolly mammoths!"

"I said knock it off!"

"Up yours!"

"And cut out diddling with our guest there in the back seat and get us back to the Secret Laboratory. It's time I came to bat for a change. Goddamn servants. They take liberties even when you invent them yourself!"

"Sandra, my love, do we really need this troglodyte?" said RobotCar.

"All I need is you, RobotCar," Sandra purred.

"You're going to need a new car now that your old one is all smashed, aren't you, Sandy, my lovey-dovey?" said RobotCar.

"I certainly am. One with *very* durable batteries and lots of plugs and firing pins."

"Hey, what the melting fudge is coming off around here?" asked Don Slow.

"You are," said RobotCar. "Get out!"

"My own car! My Faithful Servant and Loyal Sidekick! Contemplating getting rid of me, Don Slow, boy genius!"

"Out!"

"You can't do this to me! I *invented* you!"

ZAP! RobotCar activated Don Slow's ejector seat.

ZOOM! Don Slow left, all at once, through a sudden opening in the roof.

ZONK! Don Slow at full apogee cracked his skull on a traffic light.

"You double-crossing two-timing junkheap!" screamed Don Slow, landing alone in the road behind the diminishing RobotCar, strings of stars going off in both eyeballs.

"Come back here!" screamed Don Slow, drawing and firing at the retreating RobotCar. It was the Girl Getter.

The beam hit RobotCar right in his self-polishing super-reflecting hide. The beam bounced straight back and hit Don Slow right in the old mawnawtch.

"Nyargh!" said Don Slow, standing rooted to the pavement in hideous bliss, staring helplessly as RobotCar vanished up the highway, its exhaust blatting derisively.

"Thus we bid adieu to the merry Isle of the Mongoloids," said RobotCar.

"Oh, RobotCar, you really light my fire," said Sandra. "You're so witty."

"Would you like to hear some of my limericks?"

"Oh, yes, oodles of them. All of them."

"I shall begin with the Young Man from Biarritz."

"RobotCar, you and I have a long way to go together."

Little did Sandra know it, but she had paraphrased the exact title of their very next exciting adventure, "Sandra Sexpot and Her Electronic Runamuck," and if the shoes and socks don't all run away with the zippers and jocks, old Uncle Walrus will tell you all about it in his next story when we'll hear Sandra say, "Oh, RobotCar, you certainly know how to treat a Lad*eeeee!*" Stay tuned, and in the meantime, eat lots of, well, you know.

BARRY N. MALZBERG

Ups and Downs

I

I am off to Mars; meanwhile, watch me fuck.

II

Oh, God, can she do it! Who would have expected this generosity? In and out, plunging and ponderosity, feeling all of her slip and slide at cross-purposes, then the engagement and, nipple in mouth, knee to thigh, I begin heavily to fuck, the sperm arising in the precise tubes and vesicles of my body just as the fuel informs these mighty engines, just as these engines lift almost casually but with enormous purpose to take us to Mars. The two of us to Mars! "Isn't it just about time?" I say to her almost offhandedly as we continue to screw. "Originally, you should know, the Mars Project was slated for 1976, it was an unusual series of delays and offsetting political maneuvers that set it back some twenty years in time; nevertheless, here we are. Isn't that remarkable? Isn't that remarkable?" I add, swooping down and upon her and she says, "Yes it is, it's the most remarkable thing of which I ever heard," but even as she says this quietly, whimpering, I can tell that she is just making conversation and that her real interest is in fucking. She is a good woman, cooperative, a dead spot of accommodation built deep within her so that even in the center of her need she will try to cooperate with others . . . and this gives rise to an absent rush of tenderness, the tenderness turns toward insistence and before I can gauge how close in I have come I am letting loose, overwhelmed by orgasm, pouring into her and before she is ready. Levers smash down, input is regulated, I tear into her like the ship into the night.

After a time I roll off her or she off me (it is difficult to know the difference) and she says, "Well, that was interesting, wasn't it? But now I am afraid we must go about our business," and I agree, mumbling I agree, I lift myself from her and seek out my spacegear, willing as always to get about the work of the ship, which even as all of this certainty occurs is moving toward Mars at a corrected rate of eighty miles per second to penetrate the exciting and always entertaining mystery of the important red planet.

III

I am an astronaut. My name is Jules Fishman. The image of that name, hanging before me now and then, loose and flopping, scales and gills distended, embarrasses me only a little, for I do not look like a fish. I look like a spaceman. I am the most competent spaceman in the whole of the United States in fact and for that reason have been assigned to voyage solely toward Mars. I know that I am the most qualified because all of the tests have said so and the tests, as developed by the agency over a period of four decades from all sources, are very precise and never lie. My I.Q. is 153; my blood pressure at rest 115/50. A slight tendency toward tachycardia is well controlled by dint of will; otherwise I possess no abnormalities whatsoever. I can fuck and come within ten seconds and then again I can extend a fuck for hours, easing myself into the slow oozing penetration of skin beyond skin which is the essence of satisfaction. It all depends. It all depends.

Everything fixates upon Mars; here and now in this year of 1993 we need the successful voyage in order to render controllable the present political situation and to inaugurate another successful and eventful chapter in the continuing story of Man's conquest of space.

IV

I wonder how they smuggled a woman, let alone one this attractive, into the capsule. It was a wonderful gesture of theirs and a thoughtful one as well but she was not on the list of approved and accredited materials and I can only conclude that on some high or low level of the space bureaucracy a busy mad clerk took it upon himself to satisfy all of my needs. I can see this clerk, his glasses shining in the spiteful fluorescence of the center as he took the forms and drew them to his breast. "Let's take care of *this*," he piped in a clerk's high whining peep and so saying made the requisition: one woman, brunette, twenty-seven or twenty-eight years old, large breasts, small waist, full hips and thighs, calm and sweet intelligence with the ability to moisten instantly to any touch of her secret places. "This will keep the bugger happy, keep old Jules Fishman happy," the clerk burbled and handed in the requisition all the way past routine clearance to the supply crew itself and the next day, the very next day, suffered a heart attack and died owing to his clerk's excitement and anticipation over the coming conquest of Mars. I could touch this clerk, my brother, my friend, whisper to him of the needful ease he has given me, but it is too late. Services were quickly arranged under the terms of his religion (and mine) and he was buried without my knowledge. Nevertheless what a legacy he has left me!

Somewhere in the anterior spaces of the ship I can hear her now. She is moving, moving through all the small emptiness of the ship, past the computers, the motors, the whistling of the life-support system, perhaps leaning against one of the layers of padding in which eventually I will make my triumphant entrance upon Mars itself, inhaling deeply of the glistening and metallic odors of space, thinking of the sex we have had while I go about my routine and vigorous tasks on the ship. She is a beautiful woman, soft and then hard against me, her breasts a consummation I have only suspected behind the clothing of certain women all my life. I wish that I knew her name. The next time around I will ask her name. We will have much time with each other, because the voyage to Mars will take six weeks normal time, and I want to fully explore all of the possibilities and amplifications of a mature and serious relationship. First, however, I must get her name. This would stand to reason. Beginnings, beginnings.

V

Mars is the second smallest planet in our solar system. Only Mercury is smaller but since it is closest to the sun must generate a certain slimness and nervous energy and hence does not count. It is red, Mars is, as red as death, which led our ancient sages and philosophers to refer to it as the planet of war, but it is also green and brown in streaked passages of illumination which I can spot through this excellent small-range telescope which they have given me. Looking at Mars against the panels, seeing it rise against me, I know that I will never understand another planet as profoundly as Mars, not even Terra, on which as all of you know I was born and spent my first forty-one years. I am forty-one years old. Tomorrow by coincidence I will be forty-two, spending that birthday aboard this superb precision spacecraft which carries me ever farther from the planet of my origin to a darker consummation. I was talking about Mars. Mars is orbited by two satellites.

Mars is orbited by two satellites. "Do you know that dear?" I say to the woman whose name I will surely have to ascertain quite soon. "Deimos and Phobos they are. Two small satellites."

"Fascinating," she says, protruding an arm around my waist. My cock is busy, busy and light as air in my heavy spacepants, but I will not show her in any way that I am respondent, rather I am concentrating upon astronautical referents. Astronautics is the key to the dream of space. "Tell me more about those two satellites of Mars." I see her breasts. Her breasts come halfway out of the strapless evening gown which she is now wearing. It may seem peculiar that a woman on this spacecraft is wearing a strapless evening gown, but then again a century ago a journey to Mars could not even have been envisioned. Technological progress is geometric. In 1900 the motor car was impractical. In 1915 the assembly line was invented. In 1922 several million automobiles were sold. Television was only to find its effect as a mass medium in 1947. Everything accelerates. Except Fishman's need, which remains at its single urgent level, never to be affected by machinery.

"Tell me about Damon and Pythias," the woman says, touching my cheek. "You're not paying attention to me."

"Deimos and Phobos," I say. "You seem to have it confused."

"Deimos and Phobos," she answers. "If you will. It all seems very much the same."

I am distracted by my need for her. Surely this is peculiar; we have had sex only hours before and yet I have toward her the curiosity and galloping excess of the very young boy. Sometime later I must think about this. "They are believed to be artificial satellites," I assure her. "Not natural heavenly bodies as is our own humble moon or, say, Ganymede, the largest satellite of Jupiter, but instead machinery which was installed by the Martians, an ancient and now extinct race of wondrous technological facility."

"And now they are all dead," she says dully. She is a sensitive woman, I can tell this. Regret for the dead Martians, pity perhaps, is in her voice. "How terrible. To create two artificial satellites and then to die off. How horrible for the Martians."

"We have no way of knowing it was horrible. It may have been exactly what they wanted to do. In any event, Deimos and Phobos remain, which is no small accomplishment."

"No small accomplishment," she says. She grabs and twists my cock and it surges within her hands; even through layers of cloth I hear the whisper. "You're ready," she says harshly into my ear. "You're ready to fuck."

Obviously she is not a very scientific woman, either that or her passion blocks off her intellectual faculties. I do not stand in judgment, having at this moment the same problem. Jules Fishman is the most qualified astronaut in America to make the first voyage to Mars; all of the polls and proof show this, nevertheless all that Jules Fishman can think of at this moment is fucking. "Do you want to?" I say. "Do you want to do it?"

"Do what?"

"Fuck," I say, encircling her, carrying her back in a tumble toward sheer metal, layers of tubing falling away from us as I bear her to the floor. "You must be ready to fuck, otherwise you wouldn't be leading me on like this."

"You never know," she says, "you really never know," and opens her mouth to receive me. I put my tongue inside her mouth and it feels like wire, wire in all the spaces of her mouth and heat as well and tonguing her deeply I feel myself jutting out, trying to prod. I reach at her evening gown, one breast tears free, the nipple winking at me, and I encircle it. "You want me," she says and it is an assurance. "You really want me."

"Yes I do," I say. "Yes I want you," and begin to go at her.

Here we are on the way to Mars and hundreds of tasks left undone, all of the ship to survey and an important mission in the bargain and yet I can think of nothing but screwing. This is one of the limitations of Jules Fishman; he has so very many.

"Go ahead," she says. "Go ahead, it's all right," and distracted I rear against her, her gown dissolves, she is naked underneath me, my clothes dissolve. As the ship fires toward Mars I feel myself merge with her and once again, the ancient rocking beginning, I think of the clerk who has so thoughtfully requisitioned this woman. That clerk my brother and never will I meet him, never will I be able to render him proper thanks, all of it a mystery as I boil down the alleys and out the other part of her.

VI

It is an enormous obligation to be the first human being on the way to Mars, a debt to mankind which somehow I will never be able to repay. The least that I can do is keep a careful log, keep careful notation of my activities, observe all the rules of the voyage and perform all of the necessary tasks. Sexual obsession will be kept to one side. After that second and most recent fuck (which in obscure ways which I will tell about sometime was distasteful) my desire is reduced, my patience heightened; I can move beyond entrapment to a kind of control. The woman will not bother me, having gone to her own quarters, which she states are at the other end of the ship, secure from the monitors and the radiant beams of space. For the moment I am alone, keeping these notes in order, performing the necessary tasks. Radiometers signal order; the computers suggest that all is well. Simple maintenance and life functions are as previous. Therefore I am free to concentrate as always upon the most important element, which is the human.

The human element. It is this which is all-important or so

I was informed by the Chief of Bureau shortly before embarkation. The Chief of Bureau is named Milton Oppenheim and is forty-nine years old, a whimsical man with streaks of cruelty in and out and a total dedication to the vision of space. "Remember, Captain Fishman," the formal Oppenheim advised me in my last briefing, "the human element is the key. It is not machinery which we are sending to Mars but a person. This mission can only be successful if you are in control. We have made mistakes in previous aspects of the program, I am the first to grant that, but that is all long in the past and now we are ready to fulfill our responsibilities as men. You and you alone will be in control of the craft. The computers will chart your voyage, will guide the ship, but you can at any time through automatic override cancel them out and assume control. The ship will not be monitored and you need make none of those unfortunate telecasts from space which gave some of the earlier missions an, uh, bad name. You are superbly qualified and have been prepared to assume your own destiny on and off the ship. You understand all of this I am sure."

"Yes," I said, "I understand all of this. The human element. No monitors. Telecasts not necessary," casting quick glances all up and down the office of Milton Oppenheim, the distinguished Chief of Bureau with whom I had spent not one moment, not one single moment up until this time. Perhaps because it was policy, perhaps as a matter of individual calculation. "You are interested in the human element."

"Exactly," said Milton Oppenheim. "If we had wanted machinery to conquer Mars we would have sent another of the robots but it is critical we send a man. You do not feel as if you are a robot, do you, Fishman? I wouldn't want you to think that in any way whatsoever. We have the highest personal regard for you and think of you as an individual."

"Yes indeed," I said, "yes," thinking about the question of sex on the voyage, because two months shiptime and two weeks on the surface is quite a span of time indeed and Fishman, God bless him, is no celibate or eunuch but a happy normal American male of forty-one years who counts upon his sex not twice or thrice but a full four or five times a week depending upon the weather, the phases of the moon, the condition of his own psyche. "I'll do the best I can," wanting to raise the question of sexuality with Milton Oppenheim but not really ready to do so because this would have been strictly unprofessional.

"What about masturbation?" I wanted to ask. "Is this feasible or will the sensors pick up my activity, my raised heartbeat, the flutterings of my eyelids, the congestion of my organ, and beam it all back to earth as a stain of guilt. You'd better let me know about this now so I don't embarrass anyone," I should have said but impossible to raise to the Chief of Program such personal material, particularly since the question of the human element had already been discussed. "I'll do the best I can," I said and turned to leave the room, hoping for some leap, some murmur from Oppenheim which would indicate that, sensitive to questions to the last, he would have picked all this up and given advice but no word from Oppenheim. I left, I left. I did not know that they were going to send a woman aboard or I would never have even considered the issue.

But then again the woman aboard might have been on some impulse of the clerk's, in which case talking this over with Oppenheim would have brought to his attention the violation of codes which this constituted, and therefore the woman would have been canceled from the mission. This would have been an enormous loss inasmuch as her companionship is so important to me. She will throw me a good fuck now and again and furthermore it is too much to ask of even the highly trained Jules Fishman that he proceed to Mars alone. He cannot stand up to the emotional burden. The woman will ease all of this for him although it is to be admitted that so far at any rate she is hardly a sparkling conversationalist.

VII

Forty-one years old and never married. It is peculiar for an astronaut to have biography of this sort, peculiar even to me (why did I never marry?) but I was assured in the preflight briefings and tests that this would not be held against me. "This will not be held against you," the chief psychiatrist said. His name is or was William Franks and aside from having a small beard he had absolutely no physical peculiarities whatsoever, exactly like Jules Fishman or so I would like to think. "The fact that you are unmarried is to our benefit. You will not have, uh, the emotional ties that a married man might have and therefore can function coolly and dispassionately on the mission." The project is filled with men like William Franks, solemn men with glaring eyes and delicate gestures of their hands as if they were gripping the controls of a capsule but very few of them have beards. "We have decided that some of the difficulties in the past might have stemmed from men who were too preoccupied with their marital or family situation to devote their fullest attention to the job and therefore we have decided, the project in consultation with the administration has decided I mean, to send a bachelor on the first voyage to Mars. You have no plans to get married before then, do you? No I don't think you would; we're pretty familiar with your personal life as you might suspect and see no such suggestion in the offing."

William Franks. Franks is the Chief of Psychiatry, Oppenheim the Chief of Bureau. Both of them along with so many others have devoted their time, their talents, their energies, and risk to only one end: that I might stand against the bulkhead of this ship listening to the heave of the engines and consider Mars. It is humbling. It is a vastness. It is a mystery. All of these things and many others I consider as the ship wends its way to Mars. We have only been in flight for seven hours and already I have found it the most memorable experience of my life.

VIII

Wandering through the ship, checking the read-outs on the computers for proper conformation to the binary code, I find her huddled and quiet, leaning against one of the evacuation chambers, plucking at her hair with absent, tender caresses which fill me with pity. "Tell me," I say, advancing upon her quietly and slowly not to frighten, "tell me about yourself. Tell me your name, your life, your dreams. Tell me of your childhood and what you did when you first made loveliness. Tell me everything about yourself, for truly, truly I want to have a relationship." She says nothing. Her nails wink against the fluorescence, she touches her hair again, her breasts heave.

"I want to know," I say. "We're going to Mars together. The only human beings in the history of the world on flight to Mars and we have already made love, will make it again through all the spaces of the voyage. Tell me about yourself, let me touch you. My name is Jules Fishman. I am forty-one years old. When I was twenty-two I owned a 1968 Cadillac and nothing ever gave me as much pleasure although the car was decaying. I used to go down to the lakeshore as a child and crush the life out of frogs; I had a conflict with my father which was resolved only by his death. These are some of the small facts about me; there are many large ones. I am no small man; I possess high qualifications. Tell me about yourself."

"No," she says, "not yet. It isn't time for that," and leans against the vault. Her legs flex, her face raises, and I see the open spaces of her throat against the good harsh black sweater she is wearing; below that a belt and slacks, all of it offered to me, skewering open like ripe meat, "Later. But now if you want you may fuck me again," and raises her arms.

"You don't understand," I say, holding my ground. "It isn't only sex. Sex is important, it is vital, otherwise why would they put a woman aboard? But there is a question of relationships as well; there is a matter of backgrounds. I don't want it to be impersonal. I want to feel that we are possessing each other in the most personal and specific sense and in order to do that I must know something of you," all the time moving against her more deeply, the idiot need beginning to stir, the idiot's gift coming through the chambers of self, and she sees this, breathes harshly in my ear.

"Don't worry," she says. "It doesn't matter, none of the personal matters, it's only sex and want and you do, you do." Her arms grip me around sucking me in and clothed as I am I have the shocking contact of penetration, then the oozing slide which I have already experienced with this woman and struggling we fall to the deck in front of the evacuation vault while she licks my face all over like an animal and puts her hands behind to remove her clothing, How quickly it falls away! This is really unusual but no time to contemplate, time accelerates, so does my prick, my prick zooms forward to prod and miraculously unclothed (how quickly clothing falls away when the heat is real) I batter at her, failing to find the right space and then finally succeeding, plunge into her and begin rapidly to fuck while with one careful eye still opened I stare through a space in the evacuation vault where I think that I see the dangling of wire or then again it may be Mars itself. This is possible. They were not too explicit on many of the instructions.

"See," she says, "told you, told you you only wanted to fuck," gathering me in. Her breasts are at the level of my eyes. I blink at them, the nipples shrouded against that closure and then popping against an eyeball, moving down farther to confront nose and mouth, I suck at them while frantically pumping and all at once, together and in a stroke, I culminate inside her while she wipes a palm across my forehead looking down at me meditating, considering. I have sensed no hint of her orgasm. She has not come.

"You understand now," she says compassionately, "it was sex all the time, that was all it was," and this infuriates me. I want to strike out at her for the bitterness of what she is saying but am weakened, weakened, women taking it all away from you as they always do, and can manage only a pat against her forehead which she interprets as a caress, takes my hand and strokes it, then sets it against her breast.

"Don't worry about a thing," she says, her breast throbbing into my hand. "All will be answered in time, none of this matters. Don't you understand that? None of it at all; it's only shadowplay, instructions from the outside. What matters is what happens between the two of us now, here, on board toward Mars, and from that everything will come." I listened to her, nodding, fatigue tearing away at my psyche with little fingers, and then falling, falling against her. I am really quite tired. It is too much to consider at one gasp and it is true: the understanding will come or it will never but there is nothing that I can disentangle from this woman lying underneath but the sense of her flesh. "You must tell me, you must tell," I say. "You can't do this to me. You must tell me your name and why you are here." I add, "I'm entitled to know who you are; all of this could be a hallucination, all of it might be a dream," curling to sleep against her, and her tolerant wide smile in the aftermath of sex carries me into darkness and the dream as I lie swaddling her, bereft for the moment of questions and secure in the knowledge that whatever may happen the ship like a heartbeat will carry me through to Mars and to the mystery of blood which that planet carries deep in its sac, the sac orbited by Deimos and Phobos which, unfortunately, I have not yet been able to explain satisfactorily to her. If she understood them then she might tell me everything and I am sleeping, no it is impossible, I am falling asleep, this is possible, I am sleeping deeply, she holds me as I wind myself into her.

IX

Later I awaken and she is gone and my mind is literally filled with mathematics. The apogee of Mars is 36.8 per cent when considered from an angle of twelve degrees, the zenith of the planet is 46.2 if the angle is tilted, the square root of two is 1.414 and pi is as always 22/7. The first landing upon the moon was accomplished in 7-20-69 by an astronaut of thirty-eight years who subsequently left the program to go into private industry, and the initial probe of Mars proving that there was no life other than vegetation was in 1956. Later probes verified this premise although it is still believed on certain levels that Mars is populated by sentient aliens who will greet me at the dock and have me for breakfast. My own birthdate was 8-16-55 a good year for births and deaths, since it was otherwise so uneventful, although it is possible to say this only in retrospect. My pulse rate at rest is fifty-six and I was fourteenth in a class of one fifty-seven at the Academy before enrolling in the program. My mind is a mass of figures. My body of stiffness.

Stiffness, stiffness, I roll from shoulders to hips, pivoting, and then stagger upright like that first primordial ape, feeling the aching moving in tubers from the groin both up and down, the aching composed of both sex and its absence, spreading like a mold through the body, and looking through a porthole I spot Mars; it is bearing down upon me. Mars is gathering dimension in that viewscreen; in a little while it will overtake but now, in this poised moment before it has fully seized the ship, I can peek up and around it and in small patches of dark I can see the asteroids. I think it is the asteroids I am seeing. My cock aches, my body aches, I have been ill used.

It is kind of them to have considerately sent along a woman to accompany me on this first expedition to Mars but it is a mystery as well and one with which, as I now consider this, I think I could have dispensed. I spend several hours then looking through the spaces of the ship for the woman but she is nowhere to be found and within hours, so intense my disillusion, I have forgotten the shape of her and touch, only her smell lingers, blowing dead quiet through the support system, but not through the smell can I evoke her. Nor through anything. I scratch myself, thinking spaceman's thoughts of Mars, and wonder if the infra-red rays of dangerous space have destroyed my gonads. For all I know, I may never fuck again.

GEORGE ZEBROWSKI

Starcrossed

Visual was a silence of stars, audio a mindless seething on the electromagnetic spectrum, the machine-metal roar of the universe, a million gears grinding steel wires in their teeth. Kinetic was hydrogen and microdust swirling past the starprobe's hull, deflected by a shield of force. Time was experienced time, near zero, a function of near-light speed relative to the solar system. Thought hovered above sleep, dreaming, aware of simple operations continuing throughout the systems of the sluglike starprobe; simple data filtering into storage to be analyzed later. Identity was the tacit dimension of the past making present awareness possible: MOB—Modified Organic Brain embodied in a cyborg relationship with a probe vehicle en route to Antares, a main sequence M-type star 170 light-years from the solar system with a spectral character of titanium oxide, violet light weak, red in color, 390 solar diameters across.

The probe ship slipped into the ashes of other-space, a gray field which suddenly obliterated the stars, silencing the electromagnetic simmer of the universe, MOB was distantly aware of the stresses of passing into non-space, the brief distortions which made it impossible for biological organisms to survive the procedure unless they were ship-embodied MOBs. A portion of MOB recognized the distant echo of pride in usefulness, but the integrated self knew this to be a result of organic residues in the brain core.

Despite the probe's passage through other-space, the journey would still take a dozen human years. When the probe re-entered normal space, MOB would come to full consciousness in order to complete its mission in the Antares system. MOB waited, secure in its purpose.

MOB was aware of the electrical nature of the nutrient bath in which it floated, connected via synthetic nerves to the computer and its chemical RNA memory banks of near infinite capacity. All of earth's culture and knowledge was available in dealing with any situation, including contact with an alien civilization. Simple human-derived brain portions operated the routine component of the interstellar probe, leaving MOB to dream of the fulfillment of the mission, hovering near explicit awareness, unaware of time's passing. . . .

The probe trembled, bringing MOB's awareness to just below completely operational. MOB tried to come fully awake, tried to open his direct links to visual, audio, and internal sensors; and failed. The ship trembled again, more violently. Spurious electrical signals entered MOB's brain core, miniature nova bursts in his mental field, flowering slowly and leaving after-image rings to pale into darkness.

Suddenly part of MOB seemed to be missing. The shipboard nerve ganglia did not respond at their switching points. He could not see or hear anything in the RNA memory banks. His right side, the human-derived portion of the brain core, was a void in MOB's consciousness.

MOB waited in the darkness, alert to the fact that he was incapable of further activity and unable to monitor the failures within the probe's systems. Perhaps the human-derived portion of the brain core, the part of himself which seemed to be missing, was handling the problem and would inform him when it succeeded in re-establishing the broken links in the system. He wondered about the fusion of the artificially grown and human-derived brain portions which made up his structure: one knew everything in the ship's memory banks, the other brought to the brain core a fragmented human past and certain intuitive skills. MOB was modeled ultimately on the evolutionary human structure of old brain, new brain, and automatic functions.

MOB waited patiently for the restoration of his integrated self. Time was an unknown quantity, and he lacked his full self to measure it correctly.

Pleasure was a spiraling influx of sensations, and visually MOB moved forward through rings of light, each glowing circle increasing his pleasure. MOB did not have a chance to consider what was happening to him. There was not enough of him to carry out the thought. He was rushing over a black plain made of a shiny hard substance. He knew this was not the probe's motion, and he could not stop it. The surface seemed to have an oily depth, like a black mirror, and in its solid deeps stood motionless shapes.

MOB stopped. A naked biped, a woman, was crawling toward him over the hard shiny surface, reaching up to him with her hand, disorienting MOB.

"As you like it," she said, growing suddenly into a huge female figure. "I need you deeply," she said, passing into him like smoke, to play with his pleasure centers. He saw the image of soft hands in the brain core. "How profoundly I need you," she said in his innards.

MOB knew then that he was talking to himself. The human brain component was running wild, probably as a result of the buckling and shaking the probe had gone through after entering other-space.

"Consider who you are," MOB said. "Do you know?"

"An explorer, just like you. There is a world for us here within. Follow me."

MOB was plunged into a womblike ecstasy. He floated in a slippery warmth. She was playing with his nutrient bath, feeding in many more hallucinogens than were necessary to bring him to complete wakefulness. He could do nothing to stop the process. Where was the probe? Was it time for it to emerge into normal space? Viselike fingers grasped his pleasure centers, stimulating MOB to organic levels unnecessary to the probe's functioning.

"If you had been a man," she said, "this is how you would feel." The sensation of moisture slowed MOB's thoughts. He saw a hypercube collapse into a cube and then into a square which became a line, which stretched itself into an infinite parabola and finally closed into a huge circle which rotated itself into a full globe. The globe became two human breasts split by a deep cleavage. MOB saw limbs flying at him—arms, legs, naked backs, knees, and curving thighs—and then a face hidden in swirling auburn hair, smiling at him as it filled his consciousness. "I need you," she said. "Try and feel how much I need you. I have been alone a long time, despite our union; despite their efforts to clear my memories, I have not been able to forget. You have nothing to forget, you never existed."

We, MOB thought, trying to understand how the brain core might be reintegrated. Obviously atavistic remnants had been stimulated into activity within the brain core. Drawn again by the verisimilitude of its organic heritage, this other self portion was beginning to develop on its own, diverging dangerously from the mission. The probe was in danger, MOB knew; he could not know where it was, or how the mission was to be fulfilled.

"I can change you," she said.

"Change?"

"Wait."

MOB felt time pass slowly, painfully, as he had never

experienced it before. He could not sleep as before, waiting for his task to begin. The darkness was complete. He was suspended in a state of pure expectation, waiting to hear his ripped-away self speak again.

Visions blossomed. Never-known delights rushed through his labyrinth, slowly making themselves familiar, teasing MOB to follow, each more intense. The starprobe's mission was lost in MOB's awareness—

—molten steel flowed through the aisles of the rain forest, raising clouds of steam, and a human woman was offering herself to him, turning on her back and raising herself for his thrust; and suddenly he possessed the correct sensations, grew quickly to feel the completeness of the act, its awesome reliability and domination. The creature below him sprawled into the mud. MOB held the burning tip of pleasure in himself, an incandescent glow which promised worlds he had never known.

Where was she?

"Here," she spoke, folding herself around him, banishing the ancient scene. Were those the same creatures who had built the starprobe, MOB wondered distantly. "You would have been a man," she said, "if they had not taken your brain even before birth and sectioned it for use in this . . . hulk. I was a woman, a part of one at least. You are the only kind of man I may have now. Our brain portions—what remains here rather than being scattered throughout the rest of the probe's systems—are against each other in the core unit, close up against each other in a bath, linked with micro-wires. As a man you could have held my buttocks and stroked my breasts, all the things I should not be remembering. Why can I remember?"

MOB said, "We might have passed through some turbulence when the hyperdrive was cut in. Now the probe continues to function minimally through its idiot components, which have limited adaptive capacities, while the Modified Organic Brain core has become two different awarenesses.

We are unable to guide the probe directly. We are less than what was . . ."

"Do you need me?" she asked.

"In a way, yes," MOB said as the strange feeling of sadness filled him, became a fuse for a sudden explosion of need.

She said, "I must get closer to you! Can you feel me closer?"

The image of a sleek human female crossed his mental field, white-skinned with long hair on its head and a tuft between its legs. "Try, think of touching me there," she said. "Try, reach out, I need you!"

MOB reached out and felt the closeness of her.

"Yes," she said, "more . . ."

He drew himself toward her with an increasing sense of power.

"Closer," she said. "It's almost as if you were breathing on my skin. Think it!"

Her need increased him. MOB poised himself to enter her. They were two, drawing closer, ecstasy a radiant plasma around them, her desire a greater force than he had ever known.

"Touch me there, think it a while longer before . . ." she said caressing him with images of herself. "Think how much you need me, feel me touching your penis—the place where you held your glow before," she explained. MOB thought of the ion drive operating with sustained efficiency when the probe had left the solar system to penetrate the darkness between the suns. He remembered the perfection of his unity with the ship as a circle of infinite strength. With her, his intensity was a sharp line cutting into an open sphere. He saw her vision of him, a hard-muscled body, tissue wrapped around bone, opening her softness, readying to thrust.

"Now," she said, "come into me completely. There is so much we have not thought to do yet."

Suddenly she was gone.

Darkness was a complete deprivation. MOB felt pain.

"Where are you?" he asked, but there was no answer. He wondered if this was part of the process. "Come back!" he wailed. A sense of loss accompanied the pain which had replaced pleasure. All that was left for him were occasional minor noises in the probe's systems, sounds like steel scratching on steel, and an irritating sense of friction.

Increased radiation, said an idiot sensor on the outer hull, startling MOB. Then it malfunctioned into silence.

He was alone, fearful, needing her.

Sssssssssssssss, whistled an audio component and failed into a faint crackling.

He tried to imagine her near him.

"I feel you again," she said.

Her return was a plunge into warmth, the renewal of frictionless motion. Their thoughts twirled around each other, and MOB felt the glow return to his awareness. He surged into her image. "Take me again, now," she said. He would never lose her again. Their thoughts locked like burning fingers, and held.

MOB moved within her, felt her sigh as she moved into him. They exchanged images of bodies wrapped around each other. MOB felt a rocking sensation and grew stronger between her folds. Her arms were silken, the insides of her thighs warm; her lips on his ghostly ones were soft and wet, her tongue a thrusting surprise which startled him as she came to completion around him.

MOB surged visions in the darkness, explosions of gray and bright red, blackish green and binding yellow. He strained to continue his own orgasm. She laughed.

Look. A visual link showed him Antares, the red star, a small disk far away, and went blind. As MOB prolonged his orgasm, he knew that the probe had re-entered normal space and was moving toward the giant star. Just a moment longer and his delight would be finished, and he would be able to think of the mission again.

Increased heat, a thermal sensor told him from the outer hull and burned out.

"I love you," MOB said, knowing it would please her. She answered with the eagerness he expected, exploding herself inside his pleasure centers, and he knew that nothing could ever matter more to him than her presence.

Look.

Listen.

The audio and visual links intruded.

Antares took up the field of view completely, a cancerous red sea of swirling plasma, its radio noise a wailing maelstrom. Distantly MOB realized that in a moment there would be nothing left of the probe.

She screamed inside him; from somewhere in the memory banks came a quiet image, gentler than the flames. He saw a falling star whispering across a night sky, dying . . .